Enchanted

Billionaire Untamed – Tate
Billionaire Unbound – Chloe
Billionaire Undaunted – Zane
Billionaire Unknown – Blake
Billionaire Unveiled – Marcus
Billionaire Unloved – Jett

The Walker Brothers

Release!
Player
Damaged

The Sentinel Demons

A Dangerous Bargain
A Dangerous Hunger
A Dangerous Fury
A Dangerous Demon King
The Sentinel Demons – Complete Boxed Set

Big Girls and Bad Boys

The Curve Ball
The Beast Loves Curves
Curves by Design
The Curve Collection Boxed Set

The Pleasure of His Punishment:
Individual Stories or Complete Boxed Set

The Changeling Encounters

Mate of the Werewolf
The Danger of Adopting a Werewolf
All I Want for Christmas is a Werewolf
The Changeling Encounters – Complete Boxed Set

The Vampire Coalition

Ethan's Mate
Rory's Mate
Nathan's Mate
Liam's Mate
Daric's Mate
The Vampire Coalition – Complete Boxed Set

Enchanted

THE

ACCIDENTAL

BILLIONAIRES

BOOK FOUR

J.S. SCOTT

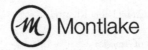

Published by Montlake, Seattle

www.apub.com

Amazon, the Amazon logo, and Montlake are trademarks of Amazon.com, Inc., or its affiliates.

ISBN-13: 9781542018906
ISBN-10: 1542018900

Cover photography and design by Laura Klynstra

Printed in the United States of America

For my husband, Sri, who was with me for our real-life adventure in Cancún. Thank you for being there with me. I'm ready to go back whenever you are!

All my love,
Jan

PROLOGUE

Noah

Seventeen years ago . . .

"You'll have to forget about being a *brother* to your siblings, Noah. From now on, you'll have to be a *parent* figure. You're all they have."

My mother's voice was little more than a whisper, but I still heard her clearly. I'd scooted my chair up next to her hospital bed because she'd wanted to have a talk.

"They still have you, Mom." My voice was hoarse and more than a little bit panicked. She wasn't *gone*. She was still *here*. She was just . . . sick.

Even as I looked at the fragile form of my only parent buried beneath a ton of white clinical bedding, I wasn't willing to let her go.

Not now.

Not ever.

My family needed her.

Hell, I *still* needed her, even though I'd just turned eighteen and had graduated from high school a few weeks earlier.

Her voice was gentle as she said, "I'm dying, Noah. You know what the doctors told you. You have to accept it now."

I clenched my fists until my knuckles were as white as the sheet they were resting on. "No," I said firmly.

I *wasn't* going to let her go. I couldn't. She'd get better. She just needed time.

"Yes," she answered. "Listen to me, Noah. I need you to be the strong one right now. You have to take care of your sisters and brothers. I don't want to leave any of you, but I'm afraid I don't have much choice."

"You have to fight," I said insistently.

"My fight is over," she said, sounding resigned as she laid her hand on top of mine. "Yours is just beginning. I'm so sorry, Noah. I never wanted you or your sisters and brothers to suffer the way you have. We've never had much. And now, things are going to get even more difficult."

"We've always had each other," I told her adamantly. "Maybe we haven't had a lot of money, but that's never mattered."

Yeah, we'd grown up poor, and my siblings were still being raised in near poverty, but they'd sure as hell never *suffered*. My mom had worked her ass off to provide the basic necessities, and now that I had a full-time job, things were bound to get easier.

If she'd just . . . get well.

Better times were ahead.

They had to be.

"I can't do this without you," I said roughly.

I couldn't ever fathom trying to be everything to my siblings. I could *never* replace my mother.

I felt a small pressure on my hand as she squeezed it weakly and whispered, "You have to, son. There isn't anyone else."

She was right. Our father had never really been in the picture, and I hadn't seen him at all for years now. And there was no other family who would claim any of us.

"Work hard, Noah. As long as you keep your head down and work, your siblings will survive. It won't be easy, but Seth and Aiden are old enough to help."

I nodded jerkily. My brothers Seth and Aiden were in high school, and they each had a part-time job to help us get by. But my twin sisters were barely into middle school, and the youngest, Owen, was just coming out of elementary.

My gut sank as I replied, "I can get another job. I can try to make more money."

I watched as she shook her head. "No matter what it costs, get your college education, Noah. Please. For me. I know it's almost an impossible task to raise your siblings, get your schooling, and still have to work full-time, but education is the only thing that's going to carry you all out of poverty. Get yourself through school, and help your siblings rise higher in life. I want you all to do better than I did."

I heard the pain in her voice, and I cringed. My entire life, I'd watched her work herself into the ground with low-paying jobs that had barely kept us fed, but she'd done it without a single complaint. "You did a good job," I told her, my voice cracking with emotion as I said it.

My siblings and I fought and gave each other a hard time, as brothers and sisters always did, but I wouldn't trade my family for anything, even if I *had* the option to be a spoiled rich kid.

Squabbling sibling stuff aside, I knew my family always had my back. And I'd always have theirs. There was no monetary value I could put on *that*. I'd rather have my family than money.

Problem was, I'd *need* cash to make sure they had everything they needed while they were growing up.

My spine stiffened, and I sat up straighter.

Time for me to man up. Mom's right. There isn't anyone else.

Like it or not, my mother *was* dying, and I *was* going to be the head of my family.

I'd been in denial for weeks, even though my mother had made it perfectly clear that there was no cure for her cancer, and that it was breaking down her body quickly. The disease was extremely aggressive, and if I had to be honest with myself, I didn't think my parent could hold on much longer.

She *wasn't* going to get better.

Our only parent was leaving us.

If I was all my siblings had, then I'd have to be realistic.

Owen, Jade, and Brooke were still just kids, and they were going to need me when Mom was gone. So I *had* to deal with the truth.

I wasn't sure if my younger siblings even really understood that their mother was probably going to be gone in a matter of days. How in the hell was I going to explain all of this to them? Hell, I hadn't come to terms with it *myself* until . . . today.

That's what this discussion is about. She's trying to make me accept that she's dying.

"You'll be all right, Noah," my mother said in a weak but soothing voice. "You've always been my good, levelheaded boy. Whether you realize it or not, you've helped me raise your younger siblings. You never really had a childhood."

That isn't really true, is it?

Yeah, I'd always had *responsibilities*, and I'd done everything I could to help my mom out with my younger siblings, but I hadn't had to do it *alone*. Mom had always made all of the hard decisions in the family. I'd just been there to babysit, pick up the kids from school, and get them fed if she was working.

"I didn't mind," I assured her.

She smiled at me. "I know. But I want you to know that I regret the fact that you never really got to be a child."

"Don't," I said desperately. Now that I was accepting the fact that she was dying, I didn't want my mother to pass away with *any* regrets. "I'd willingly die for any one of them. I'll take care of them from here," I vowed to her honestly as I squeezed her hand. "Rest easy and don't worry, Mom. I swear that I'll keep my head down and work hard, just like you said."

As terrified as I was right now, I knew I was telling my parent the truth. I'd be there for my sisters and brothers. I'd fight to keep all of us together, no matter what it took to do it. And I'd always work hard so they could survive and thrive.

At the moment, maybe I *was* overwhelmed. The thought of losing my mom was ripping my heart apart so bad that I could hardly breathe, but Mom didn't need to see *that*.

"You don't have to be brave right now, Noah. I know you're frightened," she said, like she'd just read my mind. Sometimes my mother was scary that way.

Jesus! I was going to miss her. But I was going to need to comfort my brothers and sisters. I couldn't fall apart.

"Come give your mom a hug, Noah," she whispered. "You can be strong later. Let me be here for you right now. I'm not gone yet."

I scooted my chair closer and wrapped my arms around her fragile body, laying my forehead on her shoulder. "I love you, Mom," I said, my voice hoarse with sorrow.

"I love you, too, Noah," she said in a comforting tone as she stroked her hand over my hair. "I know it doesn't feel like it right now, but everything will be okay."

I didn't know how *anything* would ever be okay again, so I wept on her shoulder as she tried to soothe me.

It was the first and last time I gave myself permission to cry.

A few days later, she was gone, and I had to stay strong and keep things normal for my brothers and sisters.

Keep your head down, work hard, and your brothers and sisters will survive.

My mother's advice became the mantra I lived by in order to keep my shit together as I took on the responsibility of caring for my siblings.

I'd made a promise to take care of them, and I'd be damned if I ever broke that vow to my mother, no matter what I had to do to keep it.

CHAPTER 1

ANDIE

The present . . .

"You have no idea how much I appreciate you doing this for me, Andie,"
Owen Sinclair said to me as I was packing for my trip to Cancún.

I threw a lightweight jacket into my suitcase and turned to him.
"I'm not just doing it for you," I reminded him. "I'm using it as an
assignment. My blog followers are always asking for more on Cancún,
and I already have a travel magazine that's more than willing to buy the
article. It's no big deal, Owen."

Like I'd refuse to do the *one* thing Owen had asked of me in all the
years we'd been friends?

Not going to happen.

Owen had been my rock during some of the darkest days of my life.
This was the first time he'd ever allowed me to do something to pay him
back for all of his friendship and support in the past.

*Really? How big of a sacrifice is it to go off to the Caribbean for a few
weeks? It doesn't even feel like I'm doing him a favor.*

A small sigh escaped from my lips as I surveyed his muscular, fit body sprawled out in all of its glory on my mattress. My suitcase was open on the chair because Owen took up a large amount of space on my bed.

The newly credentialed family-medicine doctor who was currently spread out on my quilt could easily be considered incredible eye candy, but I didn't see Owen in that way. *Yeah. Sure.* I *could* see why women salivated when they saw him, but to me, he was like the brother I'd never had.

We'd been friends since grade school, and I'd never seen Owen as anything other than a good friend who had always been there for me.

Granted, he'd changed *a lot* physically in the last year or so. The first thing he'd done, once he'd come into money, was laser surgery to fix his vision. So he no longer sported a pair of hefty glasses that obscured his gorgeous eyes.

He'd also hauled me out to help him choose a new wardrobe, something he'd never allowed me to do and pay for *before* he'd had the money to do it himself.

Another thing he'd invested in was a membership to one of the best gyms in Boston, and his body had gone from healthy but slim to deliciously muscular with the help of a personal trainer.

Owen was definitely put together differently on the surface than he had been a year ago, but unexpectedly inheriting billions of dollars hadn't changed Owen's *personality* at all.

He was still annoyingly intelligent.

He was still sweet at the most unexpected times.

He was still a jokester.

And he was still the thoughtful, insightful guy who had always been my close friend.

He's just wrapped in a more attractive package.

"So I take it you're liking your new home?" he asked with a grin. "You better be careful. The two women who owned this place before you bought it ended up married to billionaires. It might be cursed."

One of the previous owners had been Owen's sister Jade, who had ended up married to the ultrarich Eli Stone.

The other had been Riley Montgomery, who had just recently tied the knot with Owen's brother Seth.

I smiled back at him before I returned to my packing. Owen knew I wasn't looking for *that kind* of relationship at this point in my life.

I'd come back to my hometown of Citrus Beach several months ago. I'd had a nice apartment in Boston as a home base between my travels, but I'd been yearning for the temperate climate of home for a long time. I'd finally made that move and purchased the adorable cottage on the water from Riley Montgomery.

It was the first time I'd ever owned a place of my own, and the cute little house had felt like . . . home.

"Eligible Sinclair men seem to be in short supply nowadays," I said in a teasing voice. "I think your siblings and Eli Stone are the only resident billionaires in Citrus Beach."

"Hey, that doesn't mean all the good ones are *taken*," Owen said, playfully pretending he was offended. "I'm still single, and so is Noah."

I snorted. "Not happening. I plan on breaking the house curse."

Owen and I teased each other like this all the time, since neither one of us had ever been in a relationship that had been headed toward matrimony.

Owen hadn't had *time* to date during school, and I hadn't had the *inclination*.

He groaned. "I'm officially a doctor now. Are you telling me that I'm still not good enough for you?"

Owen was way too good for most women, even without a medical degree. But I wasn't about to inflate his ego. It was plenty big enough.

I rolled my eyes at him as I tossed a bathing suit into my bag. I waved at the suitcase. "Do I look like I'm ready to settle down?"

"I guess not," he said in a sullen voice as he pounded on my pillow to make it fluffier. "Can't say I'm ready to fall into domestic bliss, either. Maybe that's why we've always gotten along so well all these years."

I laughed. We'd gotten along so well because there had never been a single spark of attraction between the two of us. I didn't buy the fact that Owen wasn't ready for a serious relationship. It just hadn't happened for him . . . yet.

Both of us had been ecstatic when we'd left Citrus Beach after our high-school graduation to go to college in Boston. We hadn't really *planned* to go together. It had just worked out that way.

Unfortunately, my move to the northeast hadn't gone quite as well as Owen's had.

At least, not in the beginning.

Owen had breezed through his bachelor's degree in a little less than two years. He'd been prepared for that by taking AP classes in high school, testing out of classes, and busting his ass in summer school.

My first few years in Boston had gone a lot differently, and nothing like I'd expected. So I'd been grateful to have Owen around when I'd desperately needed his support as a friend after my entire world had fallen apart.

I rifled through my underwear drawer and added a handful of panties to my suitcase. "Have you seen Layla yet?"

Me, Owen, and Layla had hung out together in high school, but when it had come time to go to college, Layla had stayed behind to go to school in California. She and Owen would be working together now, since he planned on taking over the elderly Dr. Fortney's practice where Layla was working as a nurse practitioner.

"Not yet," Owen said flatly. "I'm sure she'll be the same pain in the ass she always was when we were in school."

"You liked her. She was our friend," I scolded him. "You two were just too . . . competitive."

"I wasn't competitive," Owen argued. "For some reason I could never understand, she just . . . changed. She wasn't even speaking to me by the time we graduated."

I turned to him and put my hands on my hips. "You and Layla were the two smartest people in our class. You *were* competitive. But I think you liked being challenged. You just won't admit it."

While Owen and I had been like brother and sister, I couldn't say the same about Layla and Owen. The three of us had been friends, but there had been enough friction between those two to send out plenty of sparks. The two of them had just never *acted* on that attraction.

"We're not kids anymore," he grumbled. "She's a professional. I'm a professional. I'm sure we won't fight like adolescents."

I smirked. I'd gotten together with Layla a lot since I'd returned to Citrus Beach. I'd made my move home and bought the cottage way before Owen's recent arrival back in California. He was going to be in for a surprise when he saw just how much Layla had grown up. Honestly, I thought that Layla would be pleasantly surprised about how Owen had matured as well. "She loves what she's doing at the clinic," I told him. "She seems happy, and God knows she *deserves* to be happy."

"I'll *have* to see her pretty soon," Owen said unhappily. "All of the paperwork is nearly done. The practice will be mine very shortly. I wonder if she knows I'm going to be her new boss."

"She knows," I informed him. Layla had sounded about as enthusiastic about the reunion with Owen as he sounded about seeing her again after all these years.

I'd spent a lot of time wondering if something had happened that I wasn't aware of, and why exactly the two friends weren't excited about seeing each other again.

Competitive or not, we *had* all been good friends.

Owen had returned to Citrus Beach less than a week ago, just in time for his brother Seth's wedding.

He was home for good now, and currently camping out at my house with most of his belongings in storage until he found a place of his own.

Not that I minded. I'd enjoyed having his company. I still wasn't completely acclimated to being back in Southern California myself, and I didn't really have many friends left here.

It had been kind of a shock to leave the frigidly cold weather in Boston for a warmer climate. "I can't say that I miss the Boston weather," I said jokingly. I'd grown up in Southern California, and I'd never gotten used to the winter climate in Massachusetts.

"Me either," Owen agreed heartily because he was a California native, too. "Winter sucked. Not that I ever got outside all that much."

I shot him a sympathetic look. He'd worked his ass off to get through medical school and then his family-practice residency. Plus, he'd always carried at least part-time work on the side until he'd very unexpectedly come into money near the end of his residency. Becoming a doctor hadn't come easily for Owen financially, and my heart had bled for him every time I'd looked at his exhausted face during those years. He might be brilliant, but there had only been so many hours in a day, and he'd used very few of them to sleep.

Not that he'd complained. *Ever.* If anything, he'd suffered from a healthy dose of guilt because his family was helping him financially to get through med school.

I'd experienced an enormous relief when Owen had become a billionaire, like all of his other siblings, because of an inheritance from his absent and long-deceased father.

I stopped packing and went to sit beside him on the bed. "It's over, Owen. Your family is wealthy now. You're a doctor, and all of your family is grown and doing well. The hard times are done."

Thank God.

Although I wasn't as rich as Owen was now, I came from money, and I'd begged him to let me help. I had a healthy bank account because of the inheritance my grandmother had left me, and I wouldn't have missed the money if the obstinate ass would have let me help him.

Stubbornly, he'd refused my assistance every time I'd offered to help him financially.

The guy had the personality of a pigheaded mule. He'd been determined to get through school or die trying without taking any handouts from friends.

It hurt me that he'd never let me do anything for *him* after he'd been there for me when I'd needed him.

Owen's emotional support had been so much more valuable than money.

He locked his hands behind his head and sat up beside me. "Maybe my siblings are happy *now*," he agreed. "All of them except Noah. As far as Noah is concerned, it's like nothing has ever *changed*. He's working himself into an early grave. I don't get him. We all have more money than we could ever possibly spend, even if we spent our entire lifetime trying. Why in the hell can't he take a break? He's lost weight, and he looks like hell. Have you seen him?"

I shook my head. "No."

"Probably because he never gets out of his damn office," Owen grumbled. "It's like he doesn't even realize that he doesn't have to work that hard anymore. Did he miss the part where we all became billionaires?"

Owen looked so troubled that I put a hand on his shoulder. "I don't know. Noah was always a workaholic," I reminded him.

"Because of us," he said anxiously. "He had siblings to support. But he doesn't have to do that anymore. Hell, my sisters had to beg him to take this vacation to Cancún we gave him for Christmas. And he owns his own business now. He doesn't take contracts. He sells his apps once they're developed. It's not like he's on a hard deadline. He can work whenever he wants, but I think he works even harder *now* than he ever has before. That punishing work schedule is starting to show. He doesn't look good."

I put an arm around his broad shoulders and bumped his arm with my head. "I'll be there for him in Cancún," I promised. I could tell that Owen was worried about his eldest brother's health.

In fact, he was so concerned that he'd asked me if I'd fly to Cancún and *force* Noah to relax. Make sure his eldest brother had leisure activities and didn't work like a maniac the entire time that Noah was in the Caribbean. I'd readily agreed since I was a blogger and travel journalist who visited locations to write about my travels and the cuisine. Yeah, I'd been to Cancún several times, but as a foodie who loved spice, I never got tired of it, and I hadn't been stretching the truth about Cancún being a popular and highly requested location for my blog and articles.

Owen kissed the top of my head in a brotherly way. "If anybody can get him to relax, it's you," he said gruffly. "Although I doubt you'll get him to do beach yoga or meditation."

"We'll see," I said in an upbeat voice, but I honestly wasn't sure I could do that, either.

Years ago, I'd idolized Noah Sinclair. He'd always seemed so grown up and wise to me. Maybe because he'd never lacked reassuring words for me as a kid and a teenager.

He'd told me I could do anything.

He'd told me he had faith in me.

He'd told me I was smart and talented.

Noah had been there to tell me everything *my parents* never had.

And I'd adored the eldest Sinclair brother for that.

Maybe I *hadn't* seen the man in close to a decade, but I'd surmised, from everything Owen had told me, that Noah hadn't changed all that much.

Back then, Noah had always worked hard to raise his siblings, but he'd also been there whenever they needed him emotionally, too. Now that I was an adult, I had to wonder who had been there for *him*.

"He's such a good man," I said with a sigh as I laid my head on Owen's shoulder. "He was always so nice to me, even though I was just your friend who hung around your place a lot. I'll find a way to make him get some rest and take some time off work. I just have to find out what he likes to do and what makes him tick."

I didn't really have a *plan* as to how I was going to get Noah away from his work. I was counting on being able to figure him out as the vacation went along.

"I don't think *he knows* what he likes," Owen contemplated. "His whole damn life has been dedicated to taking care of us."

I smiled. "I'll figure it out. Am I taking the same flight as him?"

I felt Owen nod. "Yeah. Eli offered up his jet for the trip."

I nodded. I'd momentarily forgotten that all of the Sinclairs were now among the elite group of people who had more money than they knew what to do with. After watching Owen struggle for so long, it was hard to reconcile that broke student with the wealthy man he was now.

Private jets?

Of course—why wouldn't they each have one?

Owen didn't, but he hadn't really had a lot of time to consider his newfound wealth. He'd been too busy finishing his residency.

"He doesn't mind that I'm tagging along?" I asked, wondering how Noah really felt about some friend of his kid brother's butting into his long-needed vacay.

Owen had told me very little about the Cancún trip. Only that the two-week luxury resort vacation had included a guest, and that Noah had chosen to go alone . . . until I'd agreed to go, too.

Was Noah really going to want *me* there?

Since I knew the city, Owen had begged me to go along with Noah and keep his mind off work.

I hadn't been able to refuse. Owen had *never* asked me for a favor, and I wanted to do something for him. I'd always liked Noah when I was younger, so it had sounded like a fun adventure.

Now, as I had a chance to really think about what I was doing, I had to wonder how Noah had dealt with the news that he was going to have company.

The silence stretched on, which was concerning. Owen was rarely quiet.

I disentangled myself from him just in time to see him swallow. *Hard.* "He doesn't exactly know you're going," he said sheepishly. "Yet."

CHAPTER 2

ANDIE

I was still annoyed with Owen the following day as I boarded Eli Stone's private jet. I'd discovered that Jade's husband had happily offered up his aircraft since Seth was using his own for his honeymoon with Riley in Costa Rica. The newlyweds would be returning a day or two before Noah got back from Cancún.

Once Owen had shared that he and his siblings *hadn't* told Noah that he was going to have a companion on his vacation, I'd insisted that he tell his eldest brother that I was going to be tagging along.

After all, Noah *should* have the choice of who he wanted to hang out with on his trip. I hadn't signed up to be *forced* on the poor guy.

Owen *had* reluctantly agreed to deliver the news, but I hadn't seen much of him after that. He'd gone to look at homes for sale and had stayed with Aiden last night while he was on his house hunt.

He'd *claimed* he wanted to get to know his niece, Maya, since he hadn't had the chance to spend much time with her.

I had no doubt that was *partly* the reason for Owen's absence, but I was pretty sure he also just wanted to avoid *me*.

He'd had no plans to stay anywhere other than my house *before* I'd discovered he wasn't being totally honest with me about the trip with Noah.

I didn't get angry all that often. Through meditation, yoga, and various other practices, I'd learned to control those negative emotions to a certain degree. But Owen knew me, and he'd known I was in a rare, incredibly pissed-off state of mind. I supposed he was giving me a cooling-off period before we talked again.

"Coward," I said under my breath as I climbed the stairs that led to the entrance of the aircraft.

I'd had no luck getting in touch with Owen this morning to find out how Noah was taking the news that he was going to have a companion in Cancún.

He hadn't answered my call or my texts.

So I'd just . . . showed up.

I'll play it by ear and see how everything goes. Maybe Owen did kind of set me up, but I don't have to let that ruin this whole experience. Noah needs this vacation, and apparently he needs someone to help him get out and enjoy it.

As much as I was angry about how Owen had handled the situation, I *was* still worried about Noah.

At one time, the eldest Sinclair brother had meant something to me as an older mentor.

I wasn't about to break my promise to try to get him to relax and pull his head out of his work.

Cancún was the perfect place for a person to lose themselves and shake off tension. The city was almost . . . magical.

The beautiful turquoise waters.

The warm breezes.

The gorgeous white sand.

And the food . . . OMG, *the food.*

I smiled. Generally, the cuisine was *always* a priority for me.

Just thinking about fresh fish tacos was making my mouth water, and we weren't even in the air yet.

No doubt I'd return to the US after two weeks in Mexico with *another* few extra pounds attached to my already ample hips, but it would be worth it.

Maybe it wasn't *fair* that a foodie like me tended to gain weight just by *smelling* something amazing, but it was *fact*. My already curvy body was probably about to get just a little bit curvier in the Mexican Riviera Maya.

Honestly, I'd stopped sweating the few extra pounds I carried a long time ago, so I blew off the thought of a slightly bigger ass. It was just the way my body was put together, and I loved to eat. I was fit, and that was all that mattered. Once I'd become a writer on travel cuisine, I'd given up fighting to keep the extra pounds off my hips. Truth was, I liked food way too much to worry about cutting back.

If I weighed being thinner on one side of a balance scale, and a plate of tacos on the other, the spicy food was going to win out every time.

"Welcome aboard, Ms. Lawrence," the smiling redheaded flight attendant said as I entered the jet. "My name is Nita. Let me know if there's anything I can do to make your flight with us more comfortable."

"Thank you." I smiled back at her, relieved that at least the flight crew had been notified that I was coming. "I'm excited about the trip."

"You can have a seat anywhere and fasten your seat belt. We're taking off shortly. Can I get you something to drink?" she asked.

"I can wait," I answered as I brushed by her to get into the interior of the plane.

I had an approximately six-hour flight ahead of me. I could get something after takeoff.

I stopped short as I entered the seating area, completely astounded as I looked around Eli Stone's private jet.

Holy! Shit!

My own parents were millionaires just like I was, so it wasn't like I hadn't ever flown private. On the rare occasions when I'd gone somewhere with my parents when I was younger, we'd always used a charter.

I'd just never gone private quite *like this*.

To say the aircraft was luxurious would be an understatement. The stunning décor reminded me of a luxury floating home in the sky.

There was a bar, with a table and comfy-looking chairs if one wanted to be seated at a table. The artfully arranged couches, both large and small, made up another seating area next to that one. The carpet was plush and spotless. It was a space made to be calming and comfortable for its owners.

Behind, there were reclining leather seats that would put anything first class on a commercial airliner to shame.

It was there that I saw Noah Sinclair taking up space in one of those padded recliners, his head down in his computer.

I slipped into a buttery-soft leather chair next to Noah and took a deep breath. I left one seat between us for comfort, but it really wasn't necessary since the seats were well spaced apart. It wasn't like being crammed into seats shoulder to shoulder on a commercial flight.

I loved the smell of leather, and the seat didn't disappoint. I took a deep breath and let the scent soothe me.

I adored flying, because I knew it was always going to take me away to someplace new and exciting.

I looked at Noah, astonished because he hadn't even seemed to notice my presence.

Is the man completely oblivious and deaf?

I fastened my seat belt with a lot more noise and ruckus than was really necessary for a seasoned traveler like me.

I coughed gently.

I fumbled around in my purse, looking for my e-reader.

I chatted with Nita as she passed by while we taxied.

I let out an enormous sigh when we were finally in the air, and I put my feet up in the recliner.

Nothing.

Nada.

Zilch.

It was like Noah hadn't even seen me or heard me.

He was still completely focused on his work.

"Um . . . Noah?" I said carefully.

No answer.

Louder, I queried, "Noah?"

Still nothing.

I took a moment to observe him. Even though I'd left plenty of space between the two of us, it wasn't difficult to see the signs of wear on his handsome face, but I was also mesmerized by the look of intense concentration that I'd never seen before.

Granted, I meditated, but I still had *some* awareness of my surroundings.

It was like Noah didn't notice *anything* happening around him *at all.*

How could he possibly have missed my arrival? I'd just made enough noise to wake up the dead.

Owen is right. Noah looks exhausted. Does he ever sleep? Can somebody that tightly wound actually get a decent night's rest?

I could *almost* forgive him for completely ignoring me, because I knew it wasn't about me.

He was obviously driven by some kind of personal demon to keep working without interruption.

It was like he just didn't notice . . . anything, except whatever project he was working on at the moment.

Strangely, he was dressed in a suit and tie. *Who does that when they're going to arrive in the Caribbean warmth and humidity?* He'd dumped his jacket, probably with the flight attendant, but he was definitely dressed for work.

I watched, fascinated, as his masculine fingers flew across the keyboard so fast his hands were almost a blur.

Noah's body was enormous, and he took up space. But he could use a few more pounds on his large frame.

The sleeves of his dress shirt were rolled back, probably so they didn't interfere with his ability to pound on the computer accurately. It was the *only* casual thing about his appearance.

Otherwise, he was all business.

"Noah!" I said as strongly as possible without yelling.

Oh, for God's sake, look up.

Look. Up.

Completely frustrated with his lack of response, I stretched out and slammed the laptop closed.

"What the fuck!" he grunted in protest after he'd quickly moved his fingers away from the keyboard to keep them from getting smashed. "What did you do that for?"

Okay, at least I have his attention.

"I called your name several times and you didn't answer," I explained. "Where were you?"

He reached for the top of his computer to open it again.

I reached over and put my hand firmly on top of it. "Don't you dare," I warned.

"I have work to do," he answered in an ornery tone.

"You're officially on vacation."

"Who the hell are you?" he snarled.

For a second, I was taken aback.

Had Owen not told Noah? Or did he really not recognize me?

If it was the former, I'd put a knee in Owen's balls for not explaining.

"Just consider me your tour guide," I answered.

22

Slowly, he turned his head completely in my direction to get a good look at me.

My stomach did somersaults as his eyes met mine. Noah Sinclair had always been a little intense, but the ferocity of his stare pinned me to the leather seat with no hope of escape.

Everything about Noah had obviously grown excessive over the years. Either that, or my perception of him was way different now that I was an adult.

I squirmed, but I refused to let him fluster me as he surveyed me carefully from the top of my blonde head to my toes.

He squinted a little. "Andrina?"

I swallowed hard. Obviously he had recognized me, even after ten years.

"Nobody calls me that." Well, except for my parents, and *him*. I'd let him get away with calling me by my full name when I was younger, but I wasn't a child anymore. "It's Andie."

"You were Owen's little friend. Weren't you in Boston?"

I shook my head. "Not anymore. I moved back to Citrus Beach several months ago. And I'm not exactly *little*."

For some reason, it bugged me that Noah still saw me as just *Owen's little friend*. I wasn't exactly ten years old anymore.

His dark brows narrowed as he asked, "You came back to Citrus Beach because Owen did?"

Had I returned because Owen was moving back to the West Coast? Maybe he *was* the catalyst that had gotten my ass back home, even though I'd planned on returning anyway. I'd just never seemed to have the time between my travel plans to actually move.

I nodded. "We've been best friends for years. And I've always wanted to move back."

It seemed like the easiest explanation.

Noah's full, gorgeous lips turned up slightly. "I remember. You two were inseparable. Layla was usually around both of you, too."

"Layla stayed in California. It was just me and Owen in Boston." Back then, I'd wished that Layla could join Owen and me, but I'd understood why she'd stayed local.

Noah was silent as he leaned back in his chair and continued to look me over. "You grew up," he observed. "How are your folks doing?"

I tried not to cringe, because I knew it was just a polite question. Noah really didn't know my parents.

I looked away from him. "Fine, I think. They're somewhere in the Mediterranean right now. I'm not quite sure where. I haven't heard from them for months." *That* situation wasn't unusual. My parents were rarely in Citrus Beach, even though they still maintained a home there, and generally didn't check in often.

He frowned. "I'm sorry, Andrina. It seems like they were gone a lot."

My heart missed a beat as I turned to look at him with a forced smile. "Like you said, I grew up. I'm living my own life now."

Somehow, Noah had always seemed to know that I missed my parents when I was younger. My care had pretty much been left to nannies, and then to a companion as I got older. I wasn't exactly neglected. I'd had every material thing I'd wanted.

Except . . .

"That doesn't mean that you still don't need your parents," he observed, his gorgeous hazel-eyed gaze sympathetic.

His empathy warmed my heart like it always had, but it made me uncomfortable at the same time. I still felt like Noah could see past any bravado I threw at him.

When I was a kid, it had made me feel better to talk to him.

Now that I was an adult, it was somewhat . . . disconcerting.

The way he appeared to look right through me and into the core of my being made me feel way too vulnerable. I'd spent years manufacturing a serene, relaxed, and impenetrable existence. It shook me to realize that Noah still had the same ability to probe my emotions instinctively.

When I was a child, I was glad that he appeared to understand my loneliness.

When I'd become a teen, I was pretty certain that I'd developed an enormous crush on Noah Sinclair.

Eventually, I'd gotten over the hero worship and just saw him as an older mentor, someone who'd encouraged my pursuit of a college degree as I'd gotten ready to leave for Boston to attend school.

Now, I couldn't help but see him as a *man*. A gorgeous, distracted, hardworking guy who was in desperate need of somebody to help him learn to take a deep breath.

Problem was, I hadn't counted on being so attracted to him that I could barely take a deep breath *myself.*

God, the man was overwhelmingly gorgeous. Maybe he did have dark circles under his eyes, and signs of severe stress. Yeah, he could stand to gain a few pounds, but that fact didn't detract from his tall, muscular build. His greenish-brown eyes were startling with his inky-black hair, and his whiskered jawline told me that either he'd forgotten to shave or his beard grew back lightning fast.

I let out a shaky sigh as visions of climbing into his lap and pulling that restrictive tie from his neck washed through my brain. I'd love to get him out of those stuffy clothes and . . .

Stop!

I willed my mind to get back on topic, but I wasn't quite sure what we'd been talking about *before* I started thinking lurid thoughts about my best friend's older brother. *Dammit!*

That doesn't mean you don't need your parents. Oh yeah. *That* was what he'd said.

"I'm fine with it," I squeaked as I crossed my legs uncomfortably. My X-rated daydreams had sent liquid heat directedly between my thighs. "I stay busy."

"Do you?" His earnest baritone hit a chord somewhere deep in the pit of my stomach.

His short response had felt like something incredibly sensual, which was ridiculous.

I'm going to Mexico with Noah for a reason, and my purpose is not sexual! This is all a favor to Owen. I can't let myself get distracted.

And God, I *had* gotten very preoccupied for a moment. How could I not? One look at Noah had brought forth too damn many visions of our hot, naked bodies burning up some cool cotton sheets.

"Very, very busy," I muttered, forcing my eyes away from him.

Escape! I really needed to get away from that piercing, all-knowing stare of his.

I fumbled with my seat belt and released it so I could stand up and stretch. I needed to shake off the insta-lust that had nearly devoured me whole the moment I'd gotten Noah's attention.

It wasn't real. It was just a fleeting moment of insanity.

Take a deep breath in.

Now let it out.

I stepped away so I could put some distance between me and major temptation.

I just needed to take a moment.

If I didn't get my shit together, it was going to end up being a *very long* two weeks.

CHAPTER 3

ANDIE

Breathe in.
Breathe out.

I'd kicked my shoes off, and as I moved from a yoga mountain pose into a downward dog, I realized just how much I missed my yoga pants. My jeans and the cute but short pink shirt I'd put on earlier were a little restrictive as I bent over and let my palms lie flat on the plush carpet near the bar area.

Yoga *usually* let me escape, relax, and feel more balanced. Unfortunately, even though it felt good to stretch, I could sense Noah's eyes drilling into me as I dropped my head.

"What in the hell are you doing?" he asked, sounding . . . perplexed.

"Yoga," I answered as I blew a breath out loudly. "It's good for you to get up and stretch during a long flight. It prevents blood clots and swollen feet. You should try it."

Jesus! I was babbling. Something I never did. What in the hell was wrong with me?

It was no use. There was no way I was going to be able to concentrate on clearing my mind. Not when Noah was *watching*. The best I could hope for was to relax my body.

He was silent as I moved into a couple of other positions and then flipped into a headstand, hoping we didn't hit any major turbulence that would put me down on my ass.

Breathe, Andie. Just breathe.

My body was well trained to throw off tension as I executed the poses.

My head was nearly clear when Noah finally said in a slightly awed tone, "My body doesn't quite move that way."

I moved to a cross-legged position on the floor and straightened up, hands on my thighs as I finally looked at him. "It could," I told him. "Have you ever tried to relax?"

"No. Why?" His question was rough and genuine, like the whole idea of letting go of his problems had never occurred to him.

My heart clenched just a little. Granted, the guy had some wide shoulders to take on plenty of burdens, but didn't it ever cross his mind that he could let his guard down?

It was pretty evident that it probably didn't.

"Because it's not good for you to sit in the same position for hours," I answered. "What do you do other than work?"

If I was going to figure out how to pull Noah out of his current state of mind, I had to know more about him.

"I exercise and lift in my home gym," he said defensively.

I frowned. The resort probably had a gym, but that wasn't exactly what I wanted to know. Working out was still . . . work.

"What else?" I pushed.

"I take care of my family."

Was that it? He lived and breathed work and his family?

"Hobbies?"

"None. I'm too busy for them," he answered gruffly.

"What do you do at night? After work."

"There is no *after work*," he answered sharply. "I work in the evenings, too."

I slowly got to my feet and put my hands on my hips. "Why?"

The look on Noah's face after I asked that one-word question might have been amusing if he hadn't looked so damn confused.

He looks so serious. Like he doesn't get the question.

"It's just what I do. I keep my head down and work." His expression was deadpan.

I rose to my feet and went back to my chair. "Noah, you don't have to work like that anymore. In case you missed it, you and every one of your siblings are filthy rich."

"That doesn't matter. They're always going to be my responsibility." His expression was grim as he rubbed his palms over his weary face.

Does he really believe that? "They're grown, and Owen just became a practicing physician. He's the youngest. When it comes to your family, your work is finished. You've done a good job taking care of all of them. But their happiness is *their* responsibility now, Noah."

He grumbled something incomprehensibly and frowned before he opened the lid of his laptop again.

Oh, no you don't!

I realized that what I'd said had been completely dismissed as he became absorbed in his work again.

Look up!

We'd had one golden moment of conversation, and then, like he was programmed to do it, he'd immediately and completely immersed himself in some project again.

What is he doing?

Does he truly believe that his siblings are going to remain his responsibility forever?

Maybe at one time, he'd needed to work like this, but he couldn't possibly maintain the same pace forever.

Owen had said his older brother had no life, but I probably hadn't completely believed that until *right now*.

I surveyed his expression curiously.

Does he even recognize that I'm still here?

Look up!

The guy looked almost frantic.

He wasn't just *interested* in his work. He was *obsessed*.

"What are you working on?" I asked, trying to draw him back out of himself again.

There was a silent pause, but I was relieved when he rumbled, "Dating app."

At least he wasn't *completely* oblivious to my presence.

I snorted. I couldn't help myself. "You're developing something you've probably never used?"

I didn't know it for sure, but I'd bet a delicious plate of tacos that Noah didn't make the time to use a dating app, if everything Owen had said was the truth.

Honestly, I was seeing for myself that Owen *hadn't* exaggerated.

"It will be beta tested. I don't have to use it," he said, sounding like he wasn't the least bit daunted, but he didn't deny that he never made the time to date.

I reached across the empty seat and snatched his laptop, closed it, and then slid it down between my seat and my body. "Stop, Noah. Talk to me. What have you been doing with your life since I left for college?"

Maybe his fervid stare did unnerve me, but it was better than watching him lock himself away inside of his own head.

He glared at me. "Nothing very interesting. Give the computer back."

"I'm interested," I said firmly. "We're going to be together for two weeks. I'm going to be your tour guide. I know Cancún. You're going to have a great time."

"You can go and have your fun. I'm working," he growled, a sound that probably should have sent a chill down my spine, but it didn't.

It was his now-frigid look that sent a prickle of unease through my body.

Not that I was afraid of Noah, but I was starting to get concerned that I wasn't going to be able to draw the real man out of his intimidating, workaholic form.

Something wasn't right with him.

I could feel it.

I could sense it.

And I wasn't going to ease up until *he did.*

"Give. The. Computer. Back." His tone was cold and unwavering.

I shot him my best megawatt smile. "Not until we catch up. I like to know my traveling companion. Owen did tell you I was coming, right?"

Noah shrugged his broad shoulders. "He might have. I vaguely remember him saying something about some Andy coming along. At the time, I thought you were a *male* friend of his, and I didn't care if somebody tagged along. At least this entire trip wouldn't go to waste if somebody could use it to have a good time."

His eyes had gone from cold to blank, and I wasn't sure *that* was exactly an improvement.

"It wasn't intended to go to waste. This was a gift, Noah. Use it. Your entire family will be crushed if you don't."

"Who, exactly, is going to tell them?" he drawled.

I swallowed hard. "Me. Owen is my friend. I'm not going to lie to him and tell him you had a relaxing vacay when you didn't."

I watched him as he digested the corresponding events that would take place when I told Owen the truth.

Everybody in the family would know after that, even his *sisters.*

"Stretch the truth, then, to keep them all happy," he said in a deep, guttural voice that was meant to be threatening.

Maybe that had worked to keep his siblings in line, but it wasn't working on *me*.

"No."

"Yes," he answered in a surly tone. "I don't want my sisters hurt because they think I didn't have a good time."

My spirits lifted. The Noah I once knew wasn't *completely* gone. Some of the old Noah was stuck inside that smoking-hot body of his. He'd always been sensitive to how his twin sisters felt. Seemingly, *that* hadn't changed. He was still a sucker when it came to his little sisters.

"Then I propose we compromise," I suggested. "If you relax, I'll tell them that you had a good time. They'll be happy. They're worried right now. Everyone is. It's not healthy to do nothing but work."

He let out an exasperated breath. "What the hell else is there? Work is what I know. It's what I *do*."

My heart clenched inside my chest, making it hard for me to breathe.

Didn't the man know what it was like to just spend time with the people he loved for no real reason at all?

Didn't he know how to have a little fun?

Didn't he know how to pursue his other interests, or did he not *have* any other pursuits?

Quietly, I answered him as my heart continued to ache over his conflicted expression. "There's more. There's life, Noah. Your family. Watching you continue to work this way is worrying them. Have you even been outside the country before?"

"No."

"Outside of California at all?"

"Negative."

I let out a long sigh. "Have you noticed that you have a healthy bank balance and can afford to do whatever you want now? I get that you've always had to work hard for your family, but that isn't necessary anymore."

It sounded like Noah was . . . stuck. Like he truly had no idea how to do anything except work his ass off because it was *all* he knew.

And maybe it *was* all he lived to do. That, and cater to his siblings' physical and emotional needs.

After all, he'd been doing it since he'd turned eighteen, and possibly way before his mother even passed away.

The guy had been programmed from a very young age to live to take care of his family.

Now that they were all grown and happy, maybe he *didn't* know what else to do. So he just carried on with business as usual.

Part of me wanted to weep for all of the things he'd lost, and for what he'd never had, but the bigger portion of me was determined to teach him that he was *now* capable of being a little bit selfish.

Finally, he answered, "I don't really look at my bank balance. My half brother, Evan, put most of the money into investments for me."

Ah. So for him, it isn't exactly real because he never really spends much of it. He doesn't manage it. He doesn't own it.

"I'll help you understand your portfolio." Noah needed to *see* his change in circumstances. Work with it. Make it his reality, and understand that it was very substantial, not just for him, but for all of his siblings. "I've been managing my own for years now. Do you want to hear about our itinerary for the trip?"

I'd dig deep if I had to in order to find a little bit of enthusiasm from him.

And we would go through his portfolio. Not that I'd make any changes. Evan Sinclair had a lot more investment knowledge than I did, but I was determined to make Noah's circumstances real for him.

Granted, Noah had a lot more zeros behind his numbers, but I had no doubt I could help him make the fortune substantive. He just needed to *look*.

"Not particularly," he grunted. "I don't plan on wasting time playing tourist. I have too much to get done."

His gaze was wary and intense now, but I met his stare with the stubbornness that Owen had always said was one of my best and worst assets. "You have *nothing* that can't wait. How can you have a deadline when you've never signed a contract? You haven't, right?"

"I have self-imposed deadlines," he said stoically.

That figures! Noah had always expected a lot more of himself than anybody else did.

"Change them," I insisted. "Wouldn't you rather see your sisters happy than rake in more money that you really *don't* need?"

I saw a quick glimmer of what looked like confusion on his face, and then it was gone. "It's not the money. It's security for my family."

"They already *have* security, and so do you. Now, let's make them *happy*. Lessen their worry." If I couldn't get him to be selfish at the moment, I'd use his love for his family if I had to do that to make him take a break.

Look up, Noah. For God's sake, look up.

It was like he thought that if he stopped working, he was going to jeopardize the well-being of his siblings.

What I couldn't figure out was exactly why he felt that way.

Things had changed since the time he'd needed to work like a fiend to put food on the table.

But for some reason, Noah hadn't rolled with those adjustments.

Time and a huge change in circumstances had just . . . passed him by. He hadn't paid attention to any of it.

Honestly, even if all of the siblings *hadn't* inherited an obscene amount of money, it would *still* be time for Noah to let go. His brothers and sisters were all educated or working, and all of them except Owen were married. But his youngest brother *was* now a doctor; he could certainly take care of himself.

"You're young," Noah answered stoically. "You're not thinking about your own security yet."

I crossed my arms over my chest and glared at him. "I'm not a ten-year-old kid anymore, Noah. I'm twenty-seven. Owen's age. I'm only eight years younger than you are. Of course I've thought about my security. But I have enough money to survive my entire life without working if I need to do that. I don't. I have a good career."

"Doing what, exactly?" he asked cynically.

"I have one of the biggest travel blogs in existence about travel cuisine, and I'm a freelance journalist. It pays well. It's enough that I haven't had to touch my inheritance in years. It's just growing."

"So you finished your degree?" He suddenly sounded interested in how my life had turned out.

I took a deep breath. "I didn't, actually. I had to take a break from school. After that, I traveled. I kind of fell into the whole blogger-and-journalist thing naturally."

I didn't want to talk about exactly why I'd dropped out of college, and obviously Owen hadn't broken his promise not to tell anyone, either.

Noah crossed his arms over his broad chest. "So this is a working vacation for you, too?"

I smiled because he sounded so accusatory about *me* working when *he* wasn't supposed to be doing it on vacation. "The travel part of it isn't really work for me. And this is an unexpected trip. I love food, and I love traveling. It's more of a passion. I got really lucky that way."

"And you like that? Just flitting around the world and blogging about it?" His question was more than a little condescending.

Immediately, I went on the defensive. "First of all, I don't *flit*. Generally, my trips are pretty well planned. Second, I don't think it's a crime to love what I'm doing." *Okay.* Maybe a little *too* defensive. But I hated it when people made light of my career choice. I took my responsibilities about giving travelers good information very seriously.

To his credit, he looked immediately remorseful. "I didn't really mean it that way, Andrina. I'm sorry. It's not my place to criticize what you do for a living. As long as it makes you happy."

"Andie," I said in a stiff tone, not quite ready to accept his apology. "Only my parents call me Andrina, and I've always hated it."

"Andie," he said promptly. "Now can I have my computer back?"

I rolled my eyes. So much for that brief moment of remorse after he'd pretty much implied that I was a flake.

Pushing my personal injury aside, I tried to think of a way to help Noah. He had much bigger problems than I did at the moment.

I put my hand on the cool metal edge of the laptop that was sticking out between my body and the seat. "Not quite yet," I mused. "We need to come to some kind of agreement first."

Noah shot me a pained look, but I could sense that I was about to get the first of what I hoped would be plenty of concessions on this trip. "So your plan is to basically blackmail me?" he rasped angrily.

"I'd rather think of it as an agreement between travel companions."

He glared at me. "You stole my computer, and you're threatening to tell Owen everything that happens on this trip. Blackmail."

"I'm just using what leverage I have," I said coolly. "If you won't look after yourself, then somebody should." If achieving my goals took some unsavory tactics, so be it.

He was quiet for a moment before he answered. "That's sure as hell not *your* job. It's not anybody's. I've looked after myself and my family for as long as I can remember."

Yep. That was exactly the problem. "You've done well with everybody else except yourself," I conceded.

"Give me the terms. I'll negotiate *a little*."

The tension I hadn't realized I'd been holding in every muscle of my body slowly released. He didn't sound happy, but I could live with that for now.

CHAPTER 4

NOAH

"How's Mexico?" Owen asked enthusiastically after I picked up my cell phone later that evening in my hotel suite.

I was actually glad he'd called. If he hadn't, I would have called *him*.

The little shit had gotten me into this mess; he could just get me out of it, too.

There was no damn way I was going to come out of this vacation sane if he didn't do *something*.

How's Mexico, my ass. I'd raised Owen from the time he was ten years old. I knew when he was playing at avoidance. "Did you tell me that Andrina—" *Oh, hell.* "That *Andie* was coming with me to Mexico?" I corrected.

Since my so-called tour guide was currently off checking out the resort amenities, I had a few minutes to talk before I had to worry about Andie overhearing my conversation.

"I did tell you," Owen answered in a more serious tone. "I just don't think you were paying much attention at the time."

My little brother didn't lie. Maybe he *had* told me, but he'd probably picked the perfect time to inform me. No doubt when I was working and distracted. And there were a few details he'd completely left out . . .

"I'm pretty sure you forgot to explain that *Andie* was a female."

"You knew her when she was younger," he argued. "You didn't seem all that upset about her coming along."

"I thought it was one of your *male* friends. I didn't think it was Andrina."

"She hates that name," Owen pointed out.

"I know. She made that clear on the flight over," I said in a clipped voice. "But it's the only name I've ever used for her. It's a perfectly nice name. I think you knew that I didn't know her as *Andie*."

Everything was suspect when it came to Owen right now. I knew damn well he'd breezed right over all of the details about my traveling companion.

Not that I'd planned on having any kind of company. I'd assumed any guy coming with me to Cancún would be out on the beach chasing bikini-clad females. I'd thought I could just ignore whoever tagged along.

But I sure as hell couldn't ignore the blonde-haired, blue-eyed hellion Owen had sent with me.

"Does it really matter?" he asked casually.

"We're in the same room," I complained as I looked out the big picture window in my bedroom. I had an amazing view of the Caribbean Sea. I had to admit, the water was inviting. My siblings had booked a pretty nice resort, and the suite had a great view of the beach.

"It's a suite," Owen pointed out. "It's not like you're sleeping *together*. There should be two bedrooms. If I remember right, that suite is enormous."

"There are two bedrooms," I admitted grudgingly. "I'm just not used to anybody invading my space."

Especially not a female.

"Bullshit!" Owen answered skeptically. "You're totally used to it. We grew up in a tiny house where *nobody* had any privacy. You learned to ignore it unless one of us needed something."

Okay, he had a point. But I *wasn't* used to a woman I wasn't related to sharing my space. And I was damn sure that Andie wasn't going to make it easy to ignore *her*.

She made it a point *not* to be eluded.

Andie wasn't the type of female you could just block out.

I tried not to remember how riveted I'd been as I'd watched her shapely body bending like a pretzel on the plane while she was doing . . . yoga. *Who in the hell does yoga on a flight?* Really, I wasn't sure why she did it *at all*. It sure as hell didn't look comfortable, much less relaxing. Nevertheless, I *had* been momentarily distracted, which was something I *didn't* welcome.

The woman was downright beautiful, and I couldn't stop myself from *looking*. But she was Owen's age, for God's sake.

"She wants me to *do stuff* with her," I informed him testily.

"Holy shit, Noah. That's really a nightmare. I'm so sorry I sent someone fun on this vacation with you," Owen replied drily.

I ignored the jab. "She has us booked on a private food tour tomorrow," I told him, disgusted and wanting some kind of commiseration.

If I had to be miserable, he could at least feel sorry for me.

"Sounds like fun," Owen replied. "That kind of thing is right up Andie's alley. She loves good food. Maybe she'll get you to eat something other than a sandwich at your desk."

"I happen to like sandwiches." They were convenient, easy. That was probably what I liked *most* about them.

"Try something different," he suggested. "And for God's sake, take some time off."

"I don't have much choice," I informed him stiffly. "I made a bargain with Andie, and I don't go back on my word."

"What kind of bargain?" he asked, sounding confused.

"The woman *blackmailed* me," I told him. "She told me that if I didn't take some time off, she'd make sure that Jade and Brooke knew that I worked the whole time. I had to do *something*."

Okay, maybe Andie hadn't exactly said that, but she'd made it perfectly clear that she was going to tell Owen, which was as good as just telling my two sisters. There weren't many secrets in my family.

My two twin sisters were my Achilles' heel, one of the few weaknesses I couldn't control. And Owen knew it.

The little bastard actually started to snicker as he asked, "What's the deal you made?"

"I work when she works," I explained. "If this is her *job*, I assume she'll be working for the better part of the day. She has to write blog posts, and her articles."

"Um . . . Noah . . . I hate to tell you this, but she's a pretty fast writer. I've seen her roll out a blog post to the editing stage in about an hour or two. Especially when she's excited about the topic. You're definitely not going to get away with working all day. Listen, just take the damn time off. Andie is going to find a way to get you outdoors and away from work. She's pretty damn persuasive. We've known each other most of our lives, and she was always talking me into stuff I didn't want to do when we were younger."

"What kind of stuff?" I questioned sharply.

"You're not the boss anymore, Noah. Stop thinking like you have to be the disciplinarian. Adult male here."

"Then maybe you should act like an adult," I admonished.

He chuckled. "You're just still pissed about me sending Andie with you. She's unique, Noah. You'll learn to love her company."

"She's a pest," I corrected.

"But she's nice, right? So it isn't all bad," Owen commented offhandedly.

Every muscle in my body tensed as an unwelcome thought occurred to me. "Are you two involved?"

For some damn reason, I hated the thought of Andie being intimate with my little brother.

"Hell, no. We aren't involved intimately. She's been my best friend for too damn long for me to think about her that way, and do you really think I'd send my woman off on vacation with my brother? Maybe I'm not attracted to her, but I'm not blind. She's fucking beautiful."

I had no idea why I felt relieved, but I did. "She's young," I rumbled. "I still remember when she was in pigtails."

"And you were so much older? Noah, you were barely eighteen when Mom died. I was ten. It's not like you're old enough to be my father, or Andie's, either. Come on. Admit it. Andie's gorgeous. And she's smart. Fun. You couldn't ask for a better companion."

"She's attractive," I admitted vaguely. I wasn't about to tell my little brother that his best friend had gotten my dick hard the moment I'd looked into her startling blue eyes that almost seemed to shimmer with violet tints in the right amount of light. "But she's *still* too young to say much else about her."

I was also *not* sharing the fact that since Andie was obviously so flexible, I wanted to bend her over the nearest object and nail her. I'd been trying to rationalize that instinct since the very first moment my cock had started to pay attention to Andie.

I hadn't been *successful* in making sense of that unacceptable fact . . . yet.

"There's only an eight-year age difference," Owen said, sounding frustrated. "And I wouldn't mind seeing her dating a great guy. She deserves it."

"I'm not *dating her*, Owen," I said, feeling almost panicked because I found Andie so damn attractive. "She's a travel companion. That's it."

"Okay," he said, sounding resigned. "But at least try to be a *good* travel companion for her, too. I hate the fact that she's always traveling around the world solo. Not that she's not capable of taking care of herself, but it would be nice if she had the chance to share some of her experiences with somebody else for a change."

"Why don't you travel with her?" I asked, right before my mind strangely balked at the idea.

"Maybe I will, eventually," he answered. "I've never had much time or money between work and school. Not until the inheritance happened. Now, with me taking over Dr. Fortney's practice, I'm still not going to have much time. So I'm glad she's with you right now."

A horrible thought suddenly entered my mind, and I couldn't make it go away.

"Owen, tell me you aren't trying to set me up with Andie." I knew my little brother, and he was *definitely* trying to convince me of *something* here. I had a feeling he was trying to talk me into the absurd notion that Andie and I would make a good *couple*.

"I wouldn't mind if the two of you hooked up," he answered noncommittally.

"That's insane," I ground out.

"Is it?" he asked lightly.

"Yes. Andie has turned into some kind of bohemian woman who travels the globe like she doesn't have a care in the world. She's not conventional, nor does she appear to take much of anything seriously. She stole my computer, for God's sake. We have nothing in common."

Owen was silent for a moment before he answered. "What do you want, Noah? A female who will work herself to death at a desk right next to you?"

For some reason, his comment annoyed me. "I don't need a woman. Period. I just want to get some work done."

"I have to go," Owen said abruptly. "I have a meeting with Dr. Fortney. Just be nice to Andie. You know almost nothing about her. If you think she doesn't know shit about the world and the darker side of life, you're wrong. I'll catch up with you later."

Just like that, my brother hung up.

I disconnected and shoved the phone in my pocket, still wondering what in the hell he'd meant with his last cryptic comment.

I sat down on the bed and rubbed the back of my neck, trying to ignore the beginnings of an enormous headache.

Honestly, I'd been without my computer for *hours*, so maybe I was having withdrawals.

Once I'd made that agreement to only work when she worked on the jet, Andie had refused to hand my laptop back. We hadn't talked all that much during the rest of the flight. She'd popped her earbuds in and meditated. I'd ended up falling asleep at some point, and I hadn't woken up until we were getting ready to land.

Rather than feeling refreshed, I'd been pissed at myself for nodding off like an old man.

I didn't waste time like that. Ever!

If you think she doesn't know shit about the world and the darker side of life, you're wrong.

I thought about Owen's words, wondering how in the hell Andie Lawrence could know a single thing about real life.

She'd grown up rich. The female had been privileged since the day she'd been conceived.

She'd dropped out of college.

And decided to travel around the world as a writer.

Admittedly, her parents hadn't been around as much as they should have been, but she'd been well taken care of by household staff.

I got up and headed toward the shower, hoping it would wash away my headache.

Probably what I *really* needed to do in order to feel better was to ditch my *traveling companion*.

The woman wasn't mean spirited. She never had been. I'd liked her as Owen's little friend when she was a kid.

It was just the *adult female* who Andie had become that was throwing me for a loop.

She was . . . different.

She was *not* the woman I would have expected, having known that quiet, polite child she used to be. In fact, Andie was the complete opposite of the woman I would have imagined her to be now.

It irritated the hell out of me that I somehow found that . . . *intriguing.*

Andie had been a cute kid, but she'd been shy and lacking in self-confidence, even in high school. I'd done everything I possibly could to boost her self-esteem, but I'd never been sure that it had helped much.

Holy shit, she's changed.

She certainly didn't seem unsure of herself anymore.

In fact, she seemed pretty damn secure about being a vagabond, which was curious considering she'd been an insecure kid who hadn't had any faith in herself years ago.

Now, she was a blonde-haired, blue-eyed, petite menace who was determined to change *my* lifestyle.

That sure as hell isn't happening.

Sure, maybe there *were* some things about her that kind of . . . captivated me.

Some of them were small things, like the way she flitted around like a carefree fairy, bending herself into nearly impossible yoga positions that she claimed were actually *relaxing.* She wore four little bracelets on her right wrist that jingled like tiny bells when she moved, making her seem even more like a fictional little sprite. The colorful bracelet that surrounded her other wrist didn't make a sound, but it was bright enough to make most people notice it. Notice *her.*

Maybe those little things were what made me recognize that she'd changed.

Once, she'd done everything she could not to bring attention to herself.

Now, she didn't seem to give a damn what anybody thought about her.

When she closed her eyes and appeared to block out everything around her, she'd seemed almost . . . enchanted.

Okay, maybe I *had* watched her while she was meditating, her eyes closed, her entire body and mind seemingly relaxed during the last part of the flight.

How in the hell did she manage that?

I grunted as I stripped off my clothes, turned on the shower, and stepped into the stream of hot water, every muscle in my body tense. I was fairly certain the only reason I'd fallen asleep on that plane was because I'd been watching her, deep into her meditation. The sight had eventually relaxed me enough to fall asleep.

I leaned my head back against the tile, allowing myself to picture exactly how Andie had looked, so damn sweet, so damn serene, so damn . . . fuckable.

I caught myself as my hand reached for my already rigid cock.

I opened my eyes and flipped the water to the colder side.

I am not going to get off with fantasies about that woman.

The stubborn female was a bad influence, not a wet dream.

I needed to keep my guard up and my fascination level down when it came to my travel companion.

I was a serious guy with an important job: to keep my family safe.

Keep your head down, work hard, and your brothers and sisters will survive.

That mantra was still alive and well in my head, and it was my job as the eldest in my family to keep everything . . . real. Balanced. Safe.

As soon as I got out of the shower, I was going to find a way to wrestle my computer back from the little nymph and move on with my work.

Work kept me sane.

It kept me grounded.

It kept me busy.

I needed all those things, and my family deserved the security of knowing I was still doing what I needed to do.

I didn't need a vacation.

I just needed my damn computer back.

CHAPTER 5

ANDIE

"It's just a few pieces of crickets, Noah. They aren't going to bite you. They're well roasted and very much dead," I said, exasperated by the time we'd tackled our downtown food tour the evening after our arrival.

I'd put the whole tour together last night, getting us a local guide so we could go to the downtown area for authentic food.

The hotel zone might be prettier, but the food was more Americanized there. I preferred to dive into the culture downtown for better stuff.

None of the places I'd picked were fancy. In fact, they were just the opposite. They were places where the locals ate.

Despite my irritation, I almost smiled at the sight of Noah Sinclair glaring at a taco as he held it aloft. He looked at it like the crickets were going to jump off the carne asada and attack him.

"I don't eat bugs," he answered stoically.

"Then be adventurous *today*," I replied before I took a big bite out of my own steak taco, chewed slowly, and then swallowed it. The tiny restaurant might be a hole-in-the-wall where we were forced to eat outside because of the heat, but the food was amazing. "The crickets are completely cooked. It's not like I'm asking you to pull a live, squirming, dirty slug from the ground and swallow it."

He raised a brow as his eyes shot to me. "Please tell me you haven't done that."

I shrugged. "I haven't. I do draw the line at eating anything that isn't totally dead."

Noah had done just fine at the first local restaurant we'd visited. Surprisingly, he could handle some pretty hot food, and he'd seemed to enjoy it.

I wasn't quite as successful at getting him to savor restaurant number two.

I couldn't say he'd been an enthusiastic good sport about hitting the food downtown. He'd remained mostly silent and broody. But he'd come along after I'd nagged him, so I guess I had to consider that some small sense of accomplishment.

I'd given his computer back for a while during the morning because I'd had some emails to answer, and I'd wanted to write the intro for the food blog.

He hadn't been happy when I'd snatched it back a couple of hours later.

Strangely, all it had taken was my apparent look of disappointment to get him to share this adventure with me. Granted, I'd known that his twin sisters, Brooke and Jade, could manipulate the big guy with a sad face, but I'd had no idea it would work for a woman he barely knew, too.

Not that I'd use that against him, exactly. He was obviously a sucker for a sad female face. I just hadn't realized his weakness had extended *beyond* his two younger sisters.

"Don't give me that look," he'd said back at the resort, sounding annoyed in the hotel suite earlier.

I'd asked him what *look* he was talking about.

"That *disappointed* look," he'd grumbled. "I hate that."

A few minutes later he was on his feet and joining me on the evening tour.

Good to know, but I'm not going to be a sullen woman all the time. There has to be a better way to convince him to do things.

I knew myself, and I'd feel pretty damn guilty about resorting to manipulation all the time. It wasn't my style.

Yes, we'd made a bargain about work, but I couldn't *make him* go experience Mexico with me. Our deal had only included him *not* working unless I did.

Besides, I didn't just want his physical body present, no matter how much I lusted over said body. I wanted his heart in every adventure, too.

If he wasn't enjoying himself, he'd very likely be more stressed out than relaxed.

I was yanked out of my musings when Noah shrugged his broad shoulders and shoved the taco into his mouth, taking about half the dish in one bite.

I devoured the last of my own taco as I watched him chew. His look of disgust turned to one of speculation.

"Just pretend you don't know what's on it," I advised. "It's good, right?" I asked him as he swallowed.

He shot me a wary look. "It's okay."

The rest of the taco was gone in seconds, and I smiled. It was more than just *okay*, but that was obviously all the praise I was going to get for introducing him to the local food.

"Crickets are popular here," I explained as I handed him a bottle of water I had in my tote. "They roast them and eat them like we eat chips as a snack at home."

"I refuse to consume them like potato chips," he answered grimly.

I shrugged. "I don't particularly love them straight, but they do add a little crunch to a taco."

"I tried them. Happy now?" he asked gruffly.

I beamed at him. "Very."

I hoped he hadn't decided to down the delicacy just because he thought I was disappointed.

"It actually was good. I'm glad I tried it," he said, like he was surprising *himself* by uttering those words.

It was probably the most that Noah had said to me since I'd grabbed his computer that morning. "What about the last place?" I questioned.

"Best chili relleno I've ever had," he said rather grudgingly.

Okay. That was saying a lot, considering the fact that we lived in Southern California, where the Mexican food was pretty decent.

Not surprising that he gobbled down fresh-cooked food, since Owen had told me that Noah rarely ate anything but cold sandwiches unless somebody brought him food. And lately, it appeared that he didn't eat enough of *those*, either.

"So it wasn't exactly a wasted trip?" I took another bottle of water from my tote, unscrewed the top, and chugged some down.

"Is it actually safe here? The area is a little sketchy. Although I have to say, the military guys with machine guns on the beach in the hotel zone were almost more alarming."

"Are you afraid you're going to get kidnapped?" I said jokingly.

He speared me with a look. "No. I'm more worried about *you*."

His comment was so troubled that any humor I'd been experiencing flew out the window.

I looked around. "It's different here," I explained. "The hotel zone caters to tourists. Most of Mexico's security is military. So they're just there to keep tourists safe. It just so happens that the popular military guns are automatic weapons. Don't let that bother you too much when you're at the resort. Here, we're mostly among the Mexican people. It's safe enough."

I understood that the area *did* look rough at first glance when compared to the hotel zone, where everything was sparkling sea, white-sand beaches, and luxurious resorts.

"I guess I thought the country was being taken over by the drug cartels," he said thoughtfully.

I nodded. "Unfortunately, some of the places that used to be tourist spots years ago aren't accessible anymore because of that. But Cancún is one of the safest cities in the country. We have much worse places we could go back in the US. All travel requires some common sense." I stood up and put the water bottles back in my bag. "Let's move on to dessert. I told Diego we'd meet up with him there."

Noah got to his feet, and I had to hold back a sigh as I surveyed his appearance. God, he was gorgeous. I'd convinced him to shed the suit and tie, and he looked so much more relaxed in a pair of jeans and a T-shirt.

Okay, maybe he *still* looked a bit uptight and out of sorts, but he did look a *little more* at ease.

Baby steps.

While I was hopeful that Noah would eventually have an epiphany and realize that nothing bad would happen if he stopped working, he wasn't going to change his habits or his attitude overnight.

"Where are we headed?" he questioned warily.

"El Parque de las Palapas," I explained. "It's not all that far. We can walk it. It has tons of food carts in the evening, and they have amazing churros."

He raised a brow as he fell into step with me down the darkened street. "Is the street food safe?"

"Just don't drink the water," I teased. "I've eaten a whole meal there plenty of times, and I've never gotten sick."

"I'm starting to think you have a cast-iron stomach," he muttered.

"I do," I agreed readily. "But I'm not stupid when it comes to foreign eats. I stay away from the water here. I got food poisoning in India, and I swore I'd never let it happen again. I was miserable."

"Were you all alone?" He didn't sound happy about that.

"Yes. I spent several days in hell. But I survived it. Which is why I'm determined not to let it happen again. I believe in minimal risk when I'm eating in a foreign country."

"It's not really safe for you to be traveling alone, Andie."

I didn't take offense since he sounded nothing but concerned. "It's part of my job, and I'm cautious." I wasn't about to tell him I'd made some stupid mistakes in the beginning. I was a seasoned traveler *now*, and I'd learned not to take dumb risks anymore.

Conversely, I wasn't willing to live scared, either.

Life was all about balance for me.

We walked quietly, side by side, until we reached Las Palapas. I sensed he had more to say on the subject of my solo travel, but was keeping it to himself.

The park was bright, lively, noisy with mariachi performers, and lined with street vendors selling everything from cheap souvenirs to vegetables.

I veered straight toward the churros.

Noah stopped short as a little electric car zoomed in front of him. "What are they doing?" he asked curiously as he caught up with me again.

"The kids can ride in an electric car for cheap here. Most of the adults can't afford to buy one themselves, but their kids can still get that experience," I explained. "Las Palapas is mostly locals. You'll see some tourists here, but not a lot."

I paid the vendor and handed Noah a bag of churros before I grabbed my own.

As we walked on, we both started munching on the cinnamon-and-sugar treat.

I closed my eyes for a second to savor the sweet, doughy confection as it hit my taste buds.

"They're hot," he said, sounding surprised.

I opened my eyes. "Good, right?"

He swallowed. "Fantastic, actually."

I scanned his face with a sideways glance, and I didn't miss the fact that he looked more relaxed. In fact, he almost looked like a boy as he devoured the generous order of churros.

"Go on a tour with me tomorrow," I blurted out without thinking about it. "I'm going to check out a huge cenote and tour Chichén Itzá."

I'd checked out a bunch of cenotes in Mexico, which were simply sinkholes filled in with groundwater, but I'd never been to this one. I'd never ventured out enough to see the Mayan ruins of Chichén Itzá, either.

Even though Noah hadn't exactly loosened up completely, I realized that I desperately wanted him to come with me. I wanted him to see some of the amazing sights that Mexico had to offer.

That fact had nothing to do with my promise to Owen, and everything to do with just wanting Noah's company.

I saw Diego across the park and waved to him. "There's Diego."

"Great," Noah grumbled. "Now I can watch him salivate all over you again."

I jerked my head toward him in shock. "He doesn't."

Noah grimaced. "He does. His eyes are on *you* when they should be on the damn road."

"He's a guide," I reminded him. "He wants a good tip."

"He wants to fuck you," he retorted sharply. "God, Andie, how could you miss it? The bastard was undressing you with his eyes the entire time he was looking at you."

"Don't be ridiculous. He's a married man."

"Not to mention twice your age," he added, sounding disgruntled. "Are you planning on doing this tour alone tomorrow?"

"If you won't go with me, yes. Obviously."

"I'm going," he answered firmly as we moved to meet up with Diego. "Maybe I haven't been around for your other trips, but I can make sure you get home from this one safely. Tell me that Diego isn't the tour guide."

"He's not."

"Thank God. I couldn't take an entire day and night watching *him* watch *you*. He's nauseating."

If I didn't know better, I'd almost say that Noah was jealous. I chewed on my bottom lip as I reminded myself that he was a natural protector. He was just concerned. He certainly didn't covet *me* in particular.

"It's a long trip. All day and some of the evening," I warned.

"Fine," he agreed.

My heart warmed as I glanced at him. Maybe his perception that I needed his protection was misguided, but I was going to be able to get him away from work for an entire day and most of the evening.

I was going to savor that victory, and ignore the fact that he seemed to think every guy who looked at me was thinking dirty thoughts.

Ha! Like *any* guy would really drool over my short, curvy body and overly large food-lover butt?

But I'd let Noah keep his delusions as long as it motivated him to come with me and leave his computer in our hotel suite.

CHAPTER 6

Noah

"So how did you learn to speak Spanish?" I asked Andie as we had a glass of wine together on our patio later that night.

Our current situation was a little unreal for a few reasons.

Number one . . . I didn't drink wine.

And number two . . . I didn't exactly lounge around on a patio.

Unfortunately, I couldn't get my laptop back from Andie, so it wasn't like I had anything else to do.

The heat of the day was over, and the nighttime was cooler, making the patio a very pleasant place to hang out if I was unable to work.

I'd even bought the crap Andie had fed me about a glass of red wine being good for me, so here I was.

I'd been fucking relieved to get her away from Diego. *Bullshit* that the man wasn't undressing Andie with his eyes during the whole damn tour. In fact, I was almost positive he was imagining taking her in a bunch of different positions while he was looking at her salaciously.

His intentions were crystal clear.

I probably recognized it because I couldn't help but look at her the same damn way.

Minus the creepiness of being twice her age and married, of course.

Was she really *that* clueless? The lecher had wanted more than a *good tip*. I was pretty sure he would have traded any amount of money to get Andie into the sack.

Good riddance, I'd said. I'd been elated to see the sorry bastard drive away.

If I hadn't been there, I had no doubt that the grandfather guide would have definitely put the moves on her.

He'd had no way of knowing that she *wasn't* my woman, and he'd still been bold enough to flirt with her and check her out every moment he was with us.

It had been a relief to dump the bastard when we'd gotten back to the resort. I'd wrapped my arm around Andie's shoulders and dragged her away before the idiot could try to get her number as we parted.

I made a mental note that maybe we should act more like a couple to keep the men off her.

How could she *not* have noticed that the asshole had wanted to screw her? It had been perfectly evident to *me*.

"I'm actually fluent in Spanish, French, and Italian. I also speak some German. And a smattering of other languages. I started learning as a kid, and I accelerated my learning as an adult with tutors." She made it sound like it was no big deal that she was multilingual.

To me, it was extraordinary. "That's a pretty big accomplishment."

She shrugged as she sipped her wine on the lounger right next to mine. "Not really. I always knew that I wanted to see the world. I think it's ridiculous to visit a foreign country and expect the people there to speak English. There aren't all that many regular Americans who speak an extra language fluently unless they have an immigrant parent. Why should we expect foreigners to speak English when we're visiting *their* country? If I want to play in their playground, I need to speak the language, or at least know some."

It made perfect sense, but I hadn't imagined that Andie was so accomplished. It wasn't easy to speak one foreign language, much less several.

Truth was, I really didn't know Andie at all anymore, and I knew I was about to give in to my curiosity to find out just how she'd changed.

I'd known her as a self-conscious, quiet kid. Back then, I'd done my best to encourage her, give her more self-confidence, just like I'd done with my younger siblings. But Owen had been right when he'd pointed out that she was all grown up and then some.

I didn't recognize her anymore.

But for some damn reason, I *wanted* to know her.

She fascinated the hell out of me, which I knew wasn't exactly a good thing, but I wasn't going to listen to that cautionary voice inside my head.

Andie *was* an adult. What in the hell was the harm of two adults getting to know each other?

Problem was, I wanted carnal knowledge of her, too, which scared the shit out of me. So I'd have to keep the getting-to-know-you thing casual. Indifferent. Oh, hell, strike that. I didn't feel the least bit detached when I looked at Andie, no matter how much I wanted to be.

Maybe it was because we were so different that she intrigued me.

"Tell me about what you do," I told her.

"I work and I play at the same time," she explained. "It's a great way to live."

I reached for the wine bottle and refilled my glass. If one glass was good for me, two was better, right? "You don't see your parents much?"

"Never did," she said, her voice touched with sadness. "My parents were a couple who probably never should have had a kid. I don't mean that in a bad way, but they're really wrapped up in each other and their social life. They've always been pretty absent. Not that I was abused, neglected, or anything. I lived a very privileged life that I'm grateful for, but I wish they would have been more involved in my life, especially when I was a kid. I used to envy Owen."

"Why?" I asked honestly as I refilled her glass and dropped the wine bottle back into ice. "We couldn't rub two pennies together when he was a kid. I used to feel bad because I could never afford to give much to my younger siblings."

"They had you, Aiden, and Seth," she answered in a wistful voice. "Owen was always playing ball, going to the park with one of you, or doing something with a sibling. You and your brothers were present in his life. If he had a problem, one of you was always available to talk about it. Money doesn't mean all that much, especially when you're a kid. I would have rather had a family."

Those words were spoken by a woman who had never had to count pennies in her life, but I understood what Andie meant. I'd never been *without* a lot of family, so I couldn't completely understand being in her shoes, either.

"You were lonely," I said as the truth hit me. Andie had seemed so lost as a kid because . . . she really *had been*.

Maybe she hadn't just lacked self-confidence. Belatedly, I realized that she'd had no idea where she really belonged.

"Yes."

"I'm sorry for that," I told her remorsefully.

"Don't be," she insisted. "It wasn't your job to parent me. You were basically still a kid yourself, Noah, barely eighteen, with more responsibility than any eighteen-year-old should ever have at that age. You did an amazing job. You have a great family now."

"I think so," I agreed. I was proud of everything my siblings had accomplished. But that was all *them*. It didn't have anything to do with me.

"I got through my childhood, and you helped me, Noah. I never forgot how you made the time to talk to me when I needed somebody older to give me some advice or just to tell me that I was okay."

I frowned. "I could have been around more if I'd realized how alone you were. I guess I didn't know that your parents were gone quite that often. I figured they were still in the picture *sometimes*."

It was becoming pretty obvious that Andie hadn't been a spoiled little rich girl. She'd been a lonely one whose parents weren't ever there for her. I'd had no idea that her parents had left her to her own devices year-round. I'd figured that they just sometimes had to travel for work or something.

Andie continued, "I used to blame myself for not being the kid my parents wanted, but I don't anymore. Becoming an adult means you start to see life like it really is, and not what you thought it was when you were younger. As a child, I thought they didn't want *me*, but the truth is that they didn't want to give up their lifestyle for a child. *Period.* It wouldn't have mattered if I'd been different back then. I kind of wish I hadn't spent so much time trying to twist myself into something I wasn't, just to get them to want me." She squirmed, looking uncomfortable before she changed the subject a little. "My parents like to travel, so I guess I come honestly by my own tendency to wander."

I'd gotten a quick glimpse of the vulnerable side of Andie, and I didn't want to let her shut that down, but I didn't want to make her uncomfortable, either. I decided to let it go . . . for now.

"What's it like to be in so many other cultures most of the time?" I stretched my legs out on the lounger, ready to listen—eager to listen, actually.

She might be younger, but Andie had experienced a lot more of the world than I had.

"Most of the time, it's exhilarating, but it can be exhausting. It seems like I'm always coming in and out of different time zones and trying to acclimate to how things are in different parts of the world. But

I feel grateful to have experienced all the wonderful things out there, too. I love food, so I definitely like that part of the job. I also love to blog and tell other travelers about my experiences. I think what I do is valuable. I educate people, and I can steer them away from dangerous situations, or just things that are a waste of time and their money."

"Did I insinuate that what you do isn't valuable?" I thought maybe I had.

"Pretty much," she answered as she laughed.

"I guess I was judgmental because I really don't travel."

"You should," she suggested. "You've spent the last decade or two completely dedicated to your family and their well-being. Maybe it's time for you to find yourself."

Find myself?

Find myself?

"I know who I am," I argued.

"Tell me who you are, then," she challenged, her bright-blue eyes flashing as she pinned me with an inquisitive stare.

I hesitated. "Noah Sinclair," I finally replied. "I'm a father figure, a big brother, and a techy business guy. What else is there to know?" It wasn't like I was a mysterious kind of guy.

She snorted. "That's what you are to *everyone else*. I asked you who *you* are. You have your own identity."

I wanted to tell her more. I wasn't hiding anything. Problem was, I had no idea who I was anymore. "It's not something I really think about," I said defensively. "I've never exactly had time to contemplate who I was outside of raising the family, keeping my head down, and working to make sure they were going to be okay."

"I get that." She sat up in her lounger and swung her feet to the ground beside me. "But your time is now, Noah. You don't have to worry about any of your siblings. I understand that you're pretty much programmed to put everything else aside for them. But you don't have to do that anymore. None of them *want* you to do that, because they're adults and in control of their own lives. It's time for you to think about your own life. Your family wants you to feel like you're free to do whatever you want now."

I opened my mouth to defend myself, and then closed it again to really think about what she was saying.

"I don't know how to do anything else," I finally admitted in a hoarse voice.

Hell, I hadn't thought about hobbies or where my life was going since I was a kid myself.

Keep your head down, work hard, and your brothers and sisters will survive.

I'd lived by that mantra my entire life, and it had worked. I'd never really thought about doing anything else.

I looked at Andie, and nearly fell into her gorgeous eyes. She was staring at me like I was a lost soul, and I wasn't sure I actually liked that particular expression. I didn't want her *sympathy*. At all. I needed something else entirely from her.

"I don't require saving," I said, my voice guttural. "I'm okay the way that I am. I made my mother a promise almost two decades ago, and I'm keeping it."

She reached out and laid a hand on my bicep as she questioned, "What promise did you make?"

"I told her I'd keep my head down and work so that my siblings would survive. I *had* to take over. I had no other choice. I needed to keep my word. She was dying in the hospital. There was nobody else but me. I was the only adult." My tone sounded desperate, even to my own ears.

I savored the feel of her hand on my body. Granted, I'd rather feel it in other locations, but it was good to feel . . . connected to her.

"Oh, Noah," she said softly, her eyes growing dewy and empathetic. "You've *already* kept your promise. I'm sure your mother never expected you to dedicate your entire being to them. Or your entire life. Your job is done. Your siblings are grown. All of you are wealthier than your mother could have ever dreamed about. I think your mom expected you to eventually look up and make *yourself* happy."

Had my mother expected me to eventually let go? I wasn't sure *what* her plan had been. "She died before we ever got to making a long-term plan," I told Andie. "Everything happened so fast. Her cancer was so damn aggressive. She was gone before I ever had a chance to ask any more questions. But she was right. I've kept my head down and worked all these years, and all of my siblings turned out okay. They all survived."

Her hand dropped to the arm of the lounger, and I had to admit that I missed that feeling of physical connection with her.

"They aren't just surviving," she mused. "They're thriving. And not just because of the money they inherited, either. You prepared them to live their own lives, chase their own dreams. Owen would have never been able to become a doctor if it wasn't for your emotional and financial support, and your sisters wouldn't have been able to go to college, either. All of them would have been just fine without becoming billionaires. The added family and the money were nice for everyone, I'm sure, but not essential to their happiness."

I shrugged. "I guess the whole billionaire thing has never been all that real to me. I bought a nice waterfront home so I'd be close to everybody, but then I just went back to work."

She smiled warmly, and that sweet smile made my entire body ache for a whole lot more.

"Let's make it real," she insisted as she hopped up. "Let me get your computer, and we'll look at your portfolio."

"*Now* you decide to hand back my computer," I griped.

The mischievous look she shot me as she sauntered back into the suite through the sliding glass doors made my dick stand up and take notice.

What the hell?

Why in the fuck did my body react so damn hard, *literally hard*, just from seeing Andie smile?

My head thumped back against the lounger as I held back a groan of frustration.

I'd never meant to spill my guts to Andie.

I was the one usually dishing out advice.

I didn't talk about my own emotions. Ever!

And I really had no desire to start doing it *now*.

Unfortunately, honesty poured out of my mouth every damn time I spoke to her. I couldn't seem to help myself.

Andie was like a beautiful siren who was pretty much untouchable, yet I couldn't lose the gnawing ache in my gut to reach for the impossible.

I wanted to catch her and keep her safe. And then, I wanted to fuck her until we were both so spent that we couldn't move.

Son of a bitch!

I was so . . . screwed.

"Here we go," Andie said merrily as she breezed back out onto the patio. "Find it for me, please?"

I blinked hard as I took the computer from her.

Hell, when she asked me for something in that sweet, persuasive tone that got my dick harder than a rock, I was pretty sure I'd go jump off the tallest bridge in the world if that was what she wanted me to do.

I brought up my portfolio and handed it back to her.

I tracked her movements and her expression as she plopped her gorgeous ass down on her lounger again.

Her brow furrowed as she scanned everything for a few minutes.

"What?" I asked, wondering why she was looking for so damn long.

"Nothing's wrong," she said distractedly, her eyes never leaving the numbers on the computer as she scrolled through the information. "Your investments are really, really solid, and growing like crazy."

"They should," I answered, not in the least bit interested in the numbers. I was too busy watching *her*. "My half brother is a financial genius."

I took the laptop as she passed it over. "Look through it, Noah. Those aren't just numbers on a screen. All of the properties, businesses, and investments are yours. Real money. Real assets."

I was a business guy, but since the money had never *felt* real, I'd never bothered to analyze exactly what Evan had done with my portion of the inheritance.

I'd wanted enough to buy my home. I'd gotten it, plus another ten figures or so in a money-market account I never bothered to check.

At her insistence, I looked, and my brain actually connected with reality this time.

Even in the short time that I'd had the money, it *was* growing.

"Evan did well," I muttered, distracted as I took a real look at the assets I now owned from a business perspective. "It's actually pretty overwhelming."

"It looks like Evan has been actively managing it," Andie observed. "He didn't just invest the money and leave it. He's making sure you're getting the maximum amount of growth."

Honestly, it was surreal, which was probably why I'd never really studied the portfolio after the first time I'd looked.

Andie's right. Evan has been working on my investments consistently.

There was something about going from near poverty to unbelievable wealth that had just never clicked for me. It had been almost . . . imaginary. Intangible. So unbelievable that I'd never taken it in as my new reality.

Had I thought it would eventually just disappear?

Looking at it right now was making me face the fact that all that money wasn't going anywhere.

"There's nothing you can't buy, own, or acquire with that kind of money, Noah. You do get that, right? You do understand that you don't have to work the way you do?"

How did I explain to her that the way that I worked, and the money I'd inherited, hadn't really connected . . . until now? It hadn't even made sense to me.

Later, I couldn't have explained what happened in that moment, the instant that my brain and my inheritance truly aligned.

That exact instant when I truly realized I was free to do whatever I wanted.

The second I comprehended that my job of raising my siblings really *was* done, and that they were all just as wealthy as I was, or more.

I'd kept my head down and worked for so damn long. Just like I'd promised my mother that I would. And she'd been right. My actions had kept every one of my siblings safe. I'd worked frantically, desperately, afraid that if I didn't, something bad would happen.

Finally, I looked up because I realized that I'd done everything I'd promised my mom I would do.

And when I really looked up, I was utterly and completely . . . lost.

CHAPTER 7

ANDIE

It broke my heart to see the vulnerable expression on Noah's face.

Maybe he'd needed to be shaken out of his robotic, programmed state, but that didn't mean I had to like the shattered expression in his gorgeous eyes.

Honestly, it was no wonder that he looked like he didn't know what to do. He'd spent his entire adult life, and probably most of his teen years, taking care of his family. It was really all he knew how to do, the only thing he'd had time to accomplish.

"They still need you, Noah," I said in a gentle tone. "They just don't need you to financially support them or take care of them all the time. They're adults. Aiden has his own family now, and I'm sure that the rest of them will eventually have their own families, too. I think they'll always turn to you for advice, but you aren't in control of their lives anymore. They just want you back as a brother, instead of a parent figure. They feel guilty that you've dedicated your entire life to raising and educating them. It would help if you started living for yourself now."

He looked slightly panicked as he replied, "I'd have no idea what to do except work and take care of them, even if I don't *have* to do it."

How did any guy stop doing what he'd had to do his entire life?

Noah had lived his life on autopilot because it had worked to get his siblings grown.

My heart ached as I took in his haunted look. "I know you like what you're doing. But I think you push yourself until you really aren't loving it anymore. You're *driven* to keep working."

And not in a good way. I didn't add that concern. The poor man already looked like he'd been hit by a Mack truck.

He set the laptop down on the cement beside his lounger. "Maybe I am driven to it. Hell, I'm not sure what I'm doing. For the most part, the last few decades have passed by without me really noticing."

Instinctively, I *knew* what he'd been doing. Noah had been keeping a promise to his dying mother, and he'd never looked up again. Maybe he'd been afraid to, for fear of his siblings *not* surviving if he stopped.

I wanted to comfort him, but I didn't know how.

"I wish you could see what an amazing man you really are," I told him honestly. "You raised an entire family, provided for them, cared for them, helped them grow up to be a remarkable group of men and women. You gave up *your life* to do that. There aren't many people who would. Not to the extent that you have for all these years."

"I wouldn't change what I did, and I don't feel like I've sacrificed anything."

And *that* was exactly *why* Noah Sinclair was so incredible.

He would have gladly given until his own health was at risk from doing it, yet he didn't feel like he'd done anything extraordinary.

"It's time for you to learn how to relax and please yourself," I insisted. "Find out who you really are, and embrace that. There's no better place or time than here and now to do it. You are on vacation."

I put my feet up again, closed my eyes, and just listened to the sound of the waves hitting the beach in the distance. Noah would talk if he had more to say, but I didn't want to push him too much.

Luckily, I didn't have to probe for more information at all.

"I don't have hobbies, and my friends gave up on me as a teenager because I never had time to do anything except work."

I was relieved because he was at least contemplating his life now.

"You'll make new friends," I assured him. "And you'll eventually figure out what your real interests are once you relax and think about it."

"I still have to work. I'd go crazy if I didn't."

I smirked. "I know."

"But I guess I can give this vacation thing a try, too."

"There's so much to do here," I said with a sigh. "You won't regret it."

I wasn't celebrating my victory yet.

"Like what?"

"Beach yoga?"

"Not happening." He sounded like that was nonnegotiable.

"Parasailing?"

"Maybe."

"Salsa dancing?"

"I don't dance."

I was thinking maybe I could change that if I got a few drinks into him the first time he tried. "Snorkeling?"

"Definitely. I grew up on the water, and I love it. But I haven't snorkeled since I was a kid."

I wanted to tell him that he could have a ginormous yacht and sail around the world with an entire crew if he wanted to be on the water for a while, but I didn't. Eventually, he'd figure out all that he could do with the phenomenal resources that he had. "I love to just explore every environment," I explained. "I like history, and every country has its own unique past."

"I'm down with that," he said with a spark of interest in his voice.

The way he was starting to get into doing something other than working made my heart skip a beat.

He was willing to start experiencing his own life, and I was ecstatic.

"And, of course, I eat a lot, and then write about it. I love food."

"I think I might be starting to like it myself. However, I could easily skip the bugs." There was some humor in his tone.

"I've always wanted to ride a horse on the beach," I said wistfully.

"Not a cowboy here, darlin'," he answered drily.

I laughed. I couldn't help myself. His attempt at a Southern drawl was terrible, but I appreciated his efforts to be funny.

Noah wasn't exactly a man known for his playfulness. In fact, he was way too serious.

"Thank you," I said in a genuinely grateful tone.

He turned his head to look at me, and I was struck by the intensity in his gaze. When Noah asked a question, a person got his attention. "For what?"

"For being willing to try out new things with me," I answered as my eyes met his. "I've actually never had a travel companion. I think it's going to be . . . nice."

I wasn't used to sharing *anything* I did, for the most part, and I was usually okay with being alone. But for some reason, I really wanted to be with Noah. I wanted to figure out who he was now—to know him not as a child, but as a woman.

I hadn't expected to be so attracted to him, but I couldn't deny that I wanted to get close to him, a hell of a lot closer than I was at the moment.

The man was smoking hot, but it wasn't just his physical appearance. I was drawn to him in a way I'd never been pulled toward a guy before.

Be careful, Andie. I knew I could get burned by *that* tempting flame if I got too close to it.

I simply didn't give a damn.

Bring on the burn.

Even though I had erotic dreams of rolling around in the sheets with *him*, I was pretty safe from any kind of future heartache, since he never looked at me with any kind of sensual longing in *his* gaze.

I was certain he still saw me as *Owen's little friend.*

I'd have to try like hell to keep my salacious thoughts about him to myself, because I was suffering from unrequited lust.

He suddenly grinned, and my heart started to pound so hard that I could hear it beating in my ears. God, he was gloriously appealing when he *smiled like that.*

It was all the more alluring that he had no idea just how that smile could make a woman want to drop her panties.

"What happens in Cancún stays in Cancún, right?" he joked.

I swallowed hard, wishing that we'd end up having some really dirty secrets that I'd never share with anyone else once we left.

Something hot.

Something intimate.

Something utterly wild and unforgettable.

"Yes. Of course. Just like Vegas," I agreed. "If you have one too many shots of good tequila, I'll never tell."

"I've actually never gotten drunk," he answered. "I have an occasional beer or two, but I've never gotten hammered. I've never even tried tequila."

Oh, sweet Jesus! "Do you know how badly that makes me want to see you down some really good shots?" I asked him.

Of course he'd never gotten drunk. He'd always had to keep it together for his family.

"I'm not sure I want to get drunk," he said, considering it. "I nursed Aiden and Seth through quite a few hangovers when they were younger. It didn't look like fun."

I grinned. "Lots of water, a couple of aspirin, and a tiny amount of the hair of the dog that bit you in the morning, and then a good breakfast. Works every time for me."

He let out a groan. "Please tell me you don't run around plastered in unfamiliar territory."

"I don't," I assured him. "But there is this great party-boat tour to Isla Mujeres. There's always plenty of tequila on board."

He held up a hand. "Not too much for me. Who's going to watch out for you when you overindulge?"

My heart clenched like it was in a vise. I wanted to tell him that *nobody* had ever really watched out for me like that, but I didn't want to have to explain. "I can take care of myself."

"I know you can, but you shouldn't have to do it all the time."

For some reason, I wanted to burst into tears, and I *wasn't* a crier. I had to just keep telling myself that Noah was a natural caretaker. His desire to take care of *everybody* was second nature to him.

"Those are strong words for a guy who never lets anybody take care of *him*," I scolded teasingly.

"You're trying to help me," he reminded me.

"Not really." I blew off his compliment. "I'm pretty much doing exactly what I want to do. You're just hanging out with me while I do it."

"So, is this going to make us friends?" he asked lightly.

Friends?

Oh, God, no. I wasn't sure I could be friends with a man who made me want to get him naked and find the nearest bed.

It was my knee-jerk reaction to deny that we could *ever* be friends, but for some reason, I couldn't. "Maybe," I answered in an offhanded statement.

Since we were never going to get horizontal together, maybe at least we *could* be friends. If I could get over the fact that he caused every female hormone in my body to beg for some kind of reprieve.

"I think I need to hit the mall," he mentioned thoughtfully. "I didn't really bring a lot of casual clothes."

I snorted. "Please don't tell me that you have a suitcase full of suits."

I could tell by the look on his face that he *was* guilty of packing mostly work clothing.

"Really?" I said as my eyes widened. "Who packs heavy clothing for Cancún?"

"Apparently, I do," he said with a glimmer of mischief in his eyes.

Is there anything sexier than a man who can actually laugh at himself?

I was pretty sure that there wasn't.

"They have a Walmart downtown. And if you want something nicer, a mall not far away."

He nodded. "The mall. I want to break in that black credit card that Aiden talked me into. He had to get me some kind of invitation."

There was only one black credit card that catered to the super wealthy, and the fact that he had one made me almost envious. I'd certainly never been invited to apply. "That card has some amazing perks," I said with a sigh.

He raised a brow. "Wait. Don't tell me. You're an expert on credit cards, too."

"Of course. I want people to get the best rewards when they're traveling, so I keep track. I mean, I'm not exactly the Points Guy. But my card has three times the points for dining, plane fares, and car rental. I can cash those in to go other places. I might have a nice inheritance, but I'm not stupid about spending it. Doesn't everybody want a good deal?"

"Does that mean I should shop at Walmart, then?" he asked. "It's cheaper."

"Hell, no, big guy. I'm going to help you break in that black card. We're hitting the mall."

He needed to spend some of that money. Noah had obviously always shopped in Walmart stores or thrift stores to keep within a budget.

Time for a change!

It was time that Noah Sinclair learned to spend some of those endless funds that he had, and I was just the woman to help him do it.

CHAPTER 8

NOAH

"Wouldn't it be amazing to be here in the spring or fall to see the serpent during the equinox?"

I watched Andie twirl around with her arms out wide, that colorful bracelet of hers catching the sun as she went, her excitement over being at Chichén Itzá almost contagious.

I had the sudden urge to haul her back here on one of the equinox dates so we could watch that serpent creep down the back staircase of the giant pyramid *together*.

During the equinox, when the sun was just right, the form of a serpent would appear there for a very short time to delight anybody there to see it.

Apparently, people came by the thousands to see the spectacle, and I wanted Andie and me to be two of those participants because I knew it would make her happy.

I had to admit, the ancient Mayans had been brilliant at engineering and architecture way before modern times. The skills to design the pyramid to just the right specifications to form a light-and-shadow snake figure at the equinox was astonishing. Yet they'd done it over a thousand years ago.

"It would," I finally agreed, although I was pretty sure that if we were viewing it together, I'd spend a lot of time *watching her* instead of the snake.

We were going to miss the big event by just a couple of days, but Andie and I could always come back to see it. After all, I *could* afford my own private jet.

I shook my head while I watched the light in Andie's intelligent eyes as she surveyed the pyramid and glanced around the ancient city, like she was afraid we'd missed something.

There was no coming back.

Not with *her*, anyway.

Yeah, I *was* going to savor the next twelve days in her company, but she was *Owen's* friend. Why would she want to spend any more time with me after the Cancún trip was over?

She's here to do her damn job. She's not really here to hang out with me.

Damned if that wakeup call didn't hurt just a little, but I couldn't let myself get used to being with her.

Andie was like a falling star that a guy was never going to be able to capture.

She traveled for a living.

I spent every available moment in my home office.

The two of us were complete opposites.

And I was old enough to be her . . .

Older brother?

Hell, it wasn't like I was old enough to be her *father*. Not even close. But I felt like I had a ton of miles on my body, while Andie was so damn fresh and vibrant.

I squirmed a little as I felt a droplet of sweat trail down the back of my neck.

Shit! It was hot. Chichén Itzá was definitely interesting with its rich history, but it was hotter than blue blazes out in the middle of the enormous open field. There was no shade, and the sun was high overhead.

"I'm sweating my balls off," I muttered.

She rolled her eyes in a way that said she was more amused than irritated. "I told you to wear a hat and heavy sunscreen."

Unlike me, Andie was sporting a cute floppy hat, and she'd slathered her skin with sunscreen. She managed to look cool and comfortable, even though she was standing in the direct path of the scorching sun.

She was adorable today in a light, breathable pair of blue cotton capri pants and a sleeveless shirt.

Since we hadn't been shopping yet, I'd put on my jeans and a long-sleeved button-down shirt. I'd rolled up the cuffs, but I was still hot. Thank God it wasn't summer, but the humidity was oppressive, and the direct sun was hot.

"I don't own a hat," I rumbled.

"We'll get one for you when we go shopping tomorrow. Are you ready to go?"

I nodded, and Andie and I wandered back toward the parking lot, where our private transport was waiting.

With air conditioning.

Thank God!

We didn't get much peace until we arrived back at our car. There were kids and young adults everywhere trying to sell souvenirs, and they didn't give up easily. We were hounded for the entire walk.

"Do you want some water?" Andie took off her hat, and dug into her seemingly bottomless tote bag once we'd settled into the vehicle.

"Yeah. Please." I took a bottle from her and chugged down the entire thing.

She sipped hers as she asked, "Did you enjoy yourself?"

"It was really interesting, but I'm glad I wasn't here in the summer. It was hot enough today."

She wrinkled her nose. "It is hot. It's a pretty warm day for this time of year. But at least it wasn't raining."

As I started to cool down, I could almost feel the warmth of her body next to me.

We were way too close in the smallish back seat of a vehicle that was now headed for our next destination, which was the Ik Kil cenote.

Or maybe the seat just *felt* small because it seemed like every damn moment, I got one step closer to losing my mind every time she was in the same space with me.

Andie was like bright sunlight after spending a very long time in a dark cave. I was grateful for it, but looking at it hurt like the devil.

What in the hell was it about this mesmerizing female that kept my balls in her tight little grasp?

Hell, I knew it was all wrong for me to want her this damn badly, but I couldn't seem to stop it from happening.

Stupidly, I wasn't all that sure I *wanted* to stop it.

Being with Andie made me feel more alive than I'd felt in a very long time, and feeling that happy was seductive.

My heart nearly stopped as she leaned across my lap, bringing her body into full contact with mine.

I could smell her light, flowery scent. Maybe it was just her shampoo, but my cock didn't seem to give a damn exactly *where* Andie's sexy fragrance was coming from. It was so appealing that I was hard the instant I smelled it.

She leaned back up, her head near my shoulder. "Seat belt," she muttered as she pulled it out to fasten it beside my hip. "Some drivers here can be a little bit frightening."

Little did she understand that *she* scared me a lot more than a limo driver ever could.

I wrapped an arm around her before she could move. "Andie?" I had no idea why I'd said her name. All I knew was that I didn't want her to move away.

"Yes." She sounded breathless, and her cheeks were suddenly pink, a fact I suspected had nothing to do with the sun we'd just been exposed to in the old Mayan city.

She was so close that I could feel her breath against my cheek.

Don't do it, dumbass. Don't kiss her.

I ignored my better judgment. I was way beyond any desire to listen to my common sense.

I buried my hand in her hair and pulled her closer, and then I did what I'd wanted to do since the moment she'd stolen my computer.

I choked back a groan when I absorbed the sensation of her soft, silken mouth as it fused to mine.

She tasted like sunshine and sultry temptation, and it was a combination that was completely irresistible.

I plundered her mouth because I needed to get closer to her.

That desire got even fiercer as she opened for me to go deeper. She was beckoning me inside of her, and I sure as hell wasn't going to deny either one of us.

In that moment, she was fucking mine.

Her arms wound around my neck, and she pushed her curves against my hard body. And holy hell! We fit so perfectly that it was like she was made for me.

Mine!

I was greedy, and I ran my hand up and down her back, wishing to hell we were both naked, and not in the back of a vehicle.

I wanted those generous curves beneath my fingers.

I wanted to touch every inch of her.

I wanted this woman screaming my name while I made her come.

When we finally came up for air, we were both panting. My fingers still buried in her hair, I used the silken strands to tilt her head toward me, which was an enormous *mistake.*

I could see the same longing that I was feeling reflected in her eyes, and I nearly lost it. "Andie," I said gruffly. "Don't ask me to apologize for that. I can't."

There was no way I could be sorry for what had just happened. Kissing her had been one of the best things that had ever happened to me. I sure as fuck wasn't going to regret it.

"Don't," she said with a shake of her head. "I'm not sorry, either. I wanted it just as much as you did. And neither one of us is involved with somebody else."

Hell, I highly doubted that she'd wanted it as much as *I had.* I'd wanted it pretty damn badly. And worse, it had hardly touched on all of the things I wanted from Andie Lawrence.

She moved back to her side. My hand fell out of her hair as she reached for her own seat belt and buckled up.

"I haven't been with a woman for a very long time," I confessed.

Shit! Why in the hell did I mention that?

Maybe because it was true, and I felt inept?

She shot me a confused look. "Is that why you kissed me? Because it's been a long time for you?"

I shook my head slowly. "No." I refused to lie to her. "You're the first woman who has ever made me feel this way. For fuck's sake, Andie, I'm not using you because you're a convenient female and we're on vacation."

"How do you feel?" she asked cautiously, turning her gaze away from mine.

Exhilarated.

Alive.

Fascinated.

Carefree.

And maybe . . . happy?

Hell, if this was what happiness really felt like, sign me up for more.

I was completely addicted, and probably totally fucked.

CHAPTER 9

ANDIE

There was no way in hell I was going to get through another ten days without climbing into Noah's bed one night and begging him to put me out of my hormonal misery.

Ever since that extraordinary kiss two days earlier, I was finding it very difficult to see myself as Noah's *friend*.

I yanked the earbuds from my ears as I sat cross-legged on the floor in my bedroom of the suite.

I'd been trying for the last ten minutes to clear my head with meditation.

And I'd failed for the last ten minutes to put Noah out of my mind.

It hadn't helped that I'd had one of the most erotic dreams I'd ever experienced in my life the night before.

The minute I'd closed my eyes to meditate this morning and popped in my earbuds, I hadn't heard the voice of *the guide* in my head, and I hadn't been concentrating on my breathing.

All I could focus on was visions of Noah naked, my body writhing, equally nude, on his bed while he brought me to a mind-blowing orgasm.

"Dammit!" I cursed as I got to my feet and headed for the shower.

The man was completely destroying all of my hard-won peace. All because of a single kiss.

We'd spent day three of this vacay shopping to find casual clothing for Noah. The satisfied grin that had formed on his face every time he ran that black card with another purchase haunted me.

I was giddy every time he smiled like that, and he was starting to do it often.

Yes, he worked, but he didn't appear to be frantic about it anymore. In fact, he completed what he wanted to do for the day on his computer, and set it aside without looking the least bit guilty.

I didn't have to hold his laptop hostage anymore.

He put it aside all on his own.

After we'd spent day three shopping, we went to a restaurant I'd wanted to try for dinner. The food had been mediocre, but I'd never had a better time in a restaurant in my entire life.

And God, *that* was almost criminal in my eyes. When had I *ever* been happy anywhere with so-so food?

We'd had a couple of drinks and a few shots of tequila, and he'd started telling funny stories about his younger siblings when they were growing up. I'd laughed uproariously until my side was aching, and we'd left the eatery perfectly content, even though the cuisine had only been adequate.

Yesterday had been day four, and Noah had been downright eager to get out of the suite and onto our boat for a snorkeling adventure.

I sighed. It had been one of the most memorable days of my life.

I'd probably never forget the look of contentment and happiness on his face as we'd explored the sunken shipwreck together. That whole *boyish enthusiasm* thing looked irresistibly attractive on him.

Anything I was doing with him felt like the very first time for me, because I could see it through his eyes, and pretty much *everything* was a first for him.

I stripped off the yoga pants and T-shirt I'd donned when I'd woken up, and turned on the shower.

I finished getting ready for the day in a hurry, knowing that Noah was probably already on his computer.

He was an early riser, but since he wasn't working well into the night on this trip, he was getting plenty of sleep.

After only four days of vacation, he looked a thousand times better than he had when we'd arrived.

He was eating like a man who had been half-starved for years, so I was fairly certain he'd fill out a little before it was time for us to leave Mexico.

Once I was ready, I picked up my four bangle bracelets from the dresser and shoved them over my right hand.

I didn't go anywhere without them. There wasn't a single day that I forgot to put them on. Those bracelets should have been an ominous reminder that I shouldn't be getting so entangled with Noah, but I ignored the warning as I fastened my chakra bracelet on my left wrist.

As I stepped out of my bedroom, Noah was just entering the living room from the outside door.

"You're up," he said as he shot me an adorable grin. "I just went down to work out at the gym."

I gave him a wry look. "It's almost time for breakfast. You know I'm never late for that," I reminded him.

God, he looked good. His thick, dark hair appeared to be slightly damp from a shower, and he seemed perfectly comfortable in a new pair of cargo shorts and the forest-green polo shirt he'd put on after his workout.

I'd told him to buy that shirt because it made his hazel eyes look more green than brown when he was wearing it.

He hadn't hesitated to add it to the pile he was collecting when we were shopping.

Almost like he was on cue, the waiter arrived with our breakfast, and Noah asked him to set it up out on the patio.

We'd made it a habit to fill out our breakfast order the night before and leave it on the doorknob, so we'd have breakfast when we got up in the morning.

We settled at the table outside to eat. "I'm starving," I said as I plopped my ass down at the table once room service had departed.

"Me too," Noah agreed as he snagged a piece of bacon and chewed it while he filled his plate high. "What's on the agenda for the day?"

"I hope you can drag yourself away from work for today. We're going to Xcaret, and it really is an all-day thing. I want to explore the underground caves there, and maybe swim with the dolphins. There's so much to do there that I'd love to just take off after breakfast."

He sat down with his massive plate of food. "Sounds great. I think I can manage not opening my laptop this morning."

Noah looked unperturbed as he dug into his food, and I wished so badly that Owen could see his older brother right now. No doubt, he'd be ecstatic.

I nodded as I added some scrambled eggs to my already-full plate. "Good. Maybe we can work in some of the other activities while we're there."

"As long as it isn't beach yoga or meditation, I'm pretty much game to do anything," he said gruffly.

I cringed. "How do you feel about experiencing an authentic *temazcal* ceremony?" I'd already booked it a couple of days out, but I'd been dreading telling Noah about it.

His head jerked up. "A what?"

"It's an ancient cleansing and purification ritual that helps clear your body, mind, and spirit."

"Not happening," he answered.

"Why?"

He lifted a brow. "Do I seem like an esoteric type of guy to you?"

"Not exactly," I agreed. "But I thought you were becoming open minded. Well, except for the yoga and meditation things. It does include a cenote swim at the end, and I think it would be relaxing. I don't exactly consider myself one with Mother Earth, either, but I think it would be a unique experience. I've always liked to participate in something . . . different. It's an ancient ritual of the indigenous people."

"Which includes what, exactly?" he asked, skepticism written all over his face.

I shrugged. "I can't tell you everything, since I've never done it myself. I thought we could experience it together. But I can do it alone. No big deal. I'll leave you to your work that day."

"Tell me what you do know," he insisted.

"There's a call to the ancient gods, a sweat lodge with volcanic rock, a cleansing ceremony by a shaman, and then a cooling off in a cenote. I swear, that's about all I know. But I'm willing to give it a try. It might be cheesy, but I'll never know if I don't try it. Maybe I'm not all that esoteric, either, but I'm all about *anything* that helps me relax and clears my mind of negativity. If I feel exactly the same afterward, at least I'll experience what the ancient people did."

"Not my kind of thing," Noah answered.

"I get that," I replied wistfully. "I'm not even going to try to talk you into it. If you aren't open to it, there's plenty of other things we can do together on other days."

"I thought you were a New Age type of woman," he said thoughtfully.

I shook my head. "Not at all. I practice yoga because it's good for me spiritually, as is meditation. It helped me through some of my anxiety when I was younger, and keeps me balanced now. But I am open to almost anything. And I'm very tolerant of philosophies and cultures all over the world. I have to be. I'm not there to judge when I travel. I'm there to learn. It doesn't mean that I'm going to take up practices that don't fulfill me, but there's no crime in trying to understand some that might be different from my own."

"So what exactly do you believe in?" He pinned me with an intense gaze that made me want to squirm.

"I believe in living, and letting people live their lives exactly the way they want as long as it isn't hurting anyone else. I believe in living in the moment, because the next one isn't guaranteed. I believe in being grateful for the experiences I'm given."

"What are you grateful for right now?"

"Anything and everything I do with you," I answered bluntly. I wasn't going to lie to him.

"Why?"

"Because I like being with you, Noah. My travels can be lonely sometimes. I'm usually okay exploring on my own, but sharing things with you puts a whole new spin on traveling. Like I said . . . it's nice."

He pushed his empty plate away and grabbed his mug of coffee. "I honestly can't imagine being here with anyone else. Or alone," he said in a low, thoughtful baritone. "This time is special to me, too, Andie. I doubt I would have embraced the opportunity to try new things. More than likely, if you weren't around, I'd be fighting stress headaches and wishing I was back in California."

"But you're not?" I ventured.

He shook his head. "I'm not. You've pushed my very narrow boundaries, and I'm not exactly complaining about it."

"You're finally looking up from your computer," I teased.

"Because of you," he replied sincerely. "Hell, I never even thought about most of the things we're doing right now. You're teaching me how to live outside of work. I'm seeing the world through your eyes."

I shot him a grin. "I was thinking the same thing."

He was silent for a moment before he said grudgingly, "I'll go with you to the ceremony."

"Don't," I said firmly. "Don't do it just because I asked."

"I'm not. I'll do it because I want to spend every single moment that I can with you. And I don't really give a damn what we're doing."

My heart somersaulted inside my chest. I felt exactly the same way, which was why I'd been about to change our itinerary to skip the whole ceremony. It wasn't like it was something I *needed* to do. It was more like something I'd never done before that sounded interesting. "I don't care, either. We can do something else."

He grinned. "I'm trying to be open minded."

I sighed. There were so few men like Noah, guys who were willing to jump into almost anything, even if they thought it was weird. And the fact that he was willing to do it for me amazed me.

Just to spend time with *me.*

Just to be with *me.*

Really, nobody had ever wanted to be with me *that* badly.

"I really am okay with doing something else," I told him.

"Not a chance," he refused. "When will I ever have the opportunity to sweat my balls off in some kind of sweat lodge again?" He stood. "Let's go check out those underwater caves."

I actually giggled like a teenage girl as I stood. I couldn't help myself.

CHAPTER 10

ANDIE

"Well, what's the verdict?" I asked him curiously as we sank into the blue, clear water of the cenote in the jungle after the temazcal ceremony.

A little moan of satisfaction escaped from my lips as the cool water washed over my body. I watched as Noah submerged his head.

I'd found the entire ceremony fascinating, but it had been so hot in the sweat lodge that it felt fantastic to get cooled off in the cenote.

He swiped his dripping hair back from his face after he'd surfaced. "I think I suck at blowing into conch shells and summoning the gods."

I snorted. I hadn't done much better than he had at making any kind of significant horn noise from a conch shell. "I didn't mean *that*."

I dunked my head and came up sputtering. The chill of the water was pretty bracing after the heat of the sweat lodge, so I hefted myself up on a platform beside the cenote and let just my legs dangle into the pool of deep water.

Noah swam over and rested his arms on the wooden dock right next to me.

We'd done a private ceremony, so we had the water all to ourselves. The jungle around us made it feel secluded, but I knew it was just a short walk back to the ceremony area, where we'd eat some dinner before we left.

"I feel kind of like a wet noodle," he confessed.

I smiled. "That's a good thing. That means you're relaxed."

"I don't know about that, but I do feel wiped out. I'm glad we came here. It's pretty peaceful."

I sighed and leaned my head back. "It is, right? I think you take these kinds of experiences and make them into whatever you want."

I didn't think either one of us believed we called down the gods, but for me, the ritual had been like meditation. It had cleared my mind and left me completely relaxed.

Our surroundings were beautiful, a lush jungle that was quiet except for the occasional sounds of the local wildlife.

"It's hard to believe that this vacation is half-over already," he said thoughtfully. "I was dreading it, and now I really don't want it to go too fast."

I pulled my legs out of the water and stretched out on the platform, propping my head on my hand to look at him.

"Please don't go back to business as usual once this is over," I persuaded. "You look so much better already." I couldn't stop myself from reaching out a hand and smoothing my palm over his whiskered jaw.

I'd been careful about getting too close to him after our earth-shattering kiss, but I couldn't hold back any longer. I had to *touch* him.

Somehow, I needed to make sure he was completely out of his work mode, and be certain he was never going to return to driving himself into the ground.

He reached up, grasped my hand, and just held it tightly. "I feel better," he replied, his eyes intense and full of fire as they met mine. "I used to have headaches, but I haven't experienced a single one since the day I got here."

"Migraines?" I asked curiously.

He shook his head. "I don't think so. I think it was just tension. I never really had them diagnosed. It was a bitch to try to work through one of them."

"How often?" I asked anxiously.

"Right before I got here, nearly every day."

My heart melted. *Of course* he'd never gone to the doctor. I squeezed his hand. "Oh, Noah. You ridiculous, absurd, stubborn man," I said softly. "How much longer were you planning on torturing yourself?"

He shrugged. "In my mind, I wasn't doing that. To be honest, I was just driven to finish one project and move on to the next one. I wasn't thinking, Andie."

"You were afraid if you stopped for a moment, your family wouldn't be okay?"

"Yeah," he said huskily. "It was just one huge cycle I couldn't escape, I think. Nothing else was . . . real. Even the money wasn't real in my mind. Yeah, I knew it existed. But it wasn't really *connected* to me and my need to keep working. The only thing I really thought about was my promise to my mom, and my desperation to keep it."

I had to blink back the tears that were forming in my eyes.

Noah had still been a kid himself when his mother had died. I couldn't even imagine how lost he must have felt. He'd had the weight of his entire family on his shoulders when he was barely old enough to shave. "How did you do it? How did you manage to juggle that much family responsibility, get a college degree, and work like a maniac all at the same time?"

"I didn't think about it," he answered. "Probably if I had, it would have scared the shit out of me. But I had Aiden and Seth to help with the younger ones. And they pitched in financially with full-time jobs after they got out of high school, too. I got my bachelor's degree locally. It took a while. And most of my master's was done online. It *was* a computer-science degree."

"Incredible," I said breathlessly.

"Looking back, I have to wonder how we made it during those first few years. We were all grieving Mom in our own way, and really short on money, but even Owen and the twins tried to do everything they could to keep us together. They all picked up a lot of chores they shouldn't have had to do as kids. I'm not sure how I would have done it if I hadn't had such an amazing family. It was a group effort, really. All of us took on a lot of responsibility way too young."

"So promise me that you'll have more downtime now that you're filthy rich and your family is all grown," I pressed.

"I won't promise that I'm going to become a beach bum," he teased. "I do like designing apps and programs. I really like doing my own stuff instead of somebody else's, but I'll do it in moderation. I think I'd like to take the responsibility of managing my own wealth off Evan's shoulders. He's done it for long enough. I'd have to learn a lot to take it over myself, but I'm starting to look forward to that."

I highly doubted that Evan minded. The guy was a financial wizard. But it would be good for Noah to take control of his own life. "Good idea," I encouraged.

"It's still pretty surreal. The whole money thing. Considering that Seth, Aiden, and I used to bust our asses just to put food on our table, that much money is almost a fantasy."

"It's real," I assured him. "Don't you ever check your bank balance?"

If he had, the money would probably seem a whole lot more personal to him.

"Not really. I avoided it when we were poor. We pretty much had everything stretched and calculated to our last penny. There was no point in *looking at it*."

"You'll get used to it," I teased. "Owen kind of went through the same thing when he was trying to come to grips with being one of the richest guys in the world. I'm still not sure if he's completely adjusted to it, either."

"Everyone struggled with it," he answered.

"Except you?"

"Except me," he acknowledged. "I just ignored it for a long time."

"So everyone else is over the shock, but you're just now trying to figure it out," I told him. "You'll catch up."

"Right now, I think I have more important things to do."

I frowned. I didn't want him to go back to burying himself and ignoring reality. "Like what?"

"Being with you." He reached out and ran his fingers through my wet hair. "I can't think about anything else when you're this damn close."

My heart skipped a beat as I saw the smoldering heat in his eyes. If they kept boring into me, I knew I was going to end up scorched.

Problem was, I just didn't care.

The need to be with Noah had grown so much stronger than my fears.

He vaulted out of the water and moved until he was right in front of me. "You're the only thing I see as real right now, Andie. Just this," he said in a low growl right before he rolled me onto my back and covered my upper body with his.

I shivered as I felt his hand behind my head, protecting it from smashing onto the wood. I relished the feel of his muscular body pinning mine to the dock.

I'd wanted this since the first time I'd seen him on that jet.

In fact, I'd craved it. "Noah," I said breathlessly, feeling overwhelmed, but not so much that I wanted to get away.

He lowered his head until I could feel his breath on my lips. "Don't say *no*, Andie," he said huskily.

I reached up and wrapped my arms around his neck. "I'm not saying no."

His mouth crashed down on mine, and a needy groan was music to my ears, even though I had no idea whether it had come from him, or me.

I speared my hands into his damp hair, hanging on for dear life as every bit of the desperate need I'd been experiencing for the last week poured out of me and was put into the sensual connection of our fevered embrace.

He kissed me like his life depended on it.

Fiercely.

Deeply.

And so hungrily that it stoked my own desire. I released a tormented moan against his lips.

Noah.

Oh, God, Noah.

I'd never felt as alive as I did at the moment.

I didn't want that feeling to end.

But . . . it did.

It came to a halt the instant we heard the jarring sound of a gong close to where we were trying to climb inside each other's bodies.

"Dinner," Noah rasped harshly as he retreated. He seemed more angry than happy that he was about to be fed.

"Dammit!" I whispered sharply, my heart still galloping so fast that I couldn't move.

We'd been told that the gong would sound as soon as our dinner was ready.

Our faces were only inches apart, but I could already feel the pain of the separation from Noah.

"Do you think we could convince them to give us another hour or two here?" he asked huskily, his breath warm as it caressed my cheek.

"Doubtful," I said shakily as I tightened my grip around his neck.

I didn't want to go anywhere, and I sure as hell didn't want Noah to move.

"I'm not apologizing this time, either," he said, his voice slightly irritable.

"Understood," I said softly as I smiled. "Neither am I."

I was never going to regret being close to Noah. Maybe my time with him wouldn't last, but I was determined to enjoy it while I could.

He lowered his head and gave me a quick kiss, and then stood and pulled me to my feet. "Food, woman. We haven't eaten since breakfast."

I'd completely lost my appetite for anything except him, but I knew once I got my head together, I'd be more than grateful for some food.

Neither one of us uttered a word as we walked, hand in hand, down the path to where our dinner was about to be served.

CHAPTER 11

NOAH

After the day of the temazcal ceremony, I was done fighting the fact that I wanted Andie.

I wasn't even able to *pretend* that I didn't want to haul her to bed and fuck her until we were both completely satisfied.

The woman was mine.

She'd sealed her fate the moment she'd refused to deny me that kiss at the cenote.

Any protests I'd had when we first started the vacation were unimportant.

So what if she was eight years younger than I was?

No big deal if we were two complete opposites.

The only thing that seemed to matter to me was the burning fire in my gut that *insisted* that I claim the woman who kept my dick hard almost every moment of the goddamn day.

"Are you ready to try out the parasailing?" Andie murmured, her words garbled because her face was pressed against my shoulder.

We'd had an amazing time taking the private yacht over to Isla Mujeres. Andie had dumped the idea of a party boat, and we'd opted to explore the island on our own.

I had downed plenty of tequila after we'd returned the golf cart we'd used to tool around the island.

Now we were resting on a hammock built for two on board the yacht, and I wasn't sure I was ready to move.

I had what I wanted: Andie's body pressed against the entire length of mine.

Maybe it was both torture and bliss, but I chose to focus on the *bliss* part of the whole experience. She tormented me just by being in the same room. I might as well get some kind of satisfaction out of having her this close.

"In a little while." I kissed the top of her head.

Yeah, I *was* going to let the crew strap me into a flimsy seat that was going to take us soaring up into the sky and out over the water.

If Andie wanted it, I'd do just about anything she asked me to do.

As long as it meant that she'd be happy, laughing, and smiling.

I was just *that far gone* when it came to her. I wasn't completely averse to parasailing. In fact, I thought it would be fun.

I just didn't want to lose the sensation of her body pressed up against mine like it was at the moment.

Mine! I tightened my arm around her shoulders reflexively.

I had no idea how I'd ended up needing this woman so damn badly, but I wasn't even going to question it anymore.

My sole purpose was to ensure that I never had to live *without* her again.

The bohemian, whimsical, live-in-the-moment-and-enjoy-it female belonged with me. Andie had turned my world upside down from the moment she'd snatched my computer away, and I didn't plan on going back to the robotic workaholic I'd been before.

I couldn't.

Not as long as she was around to remind me that there was life outside of working and worrying about my family.

I'd already put aside my latest project for a week, and nothing earth shattering had happened because of it.

Honestly, I was enjoying my hedonistic vacation. The only person I was worried about pleasing was Andie, and that was working just fine for me.

I'd knocked off work, and I was still filthy rich. Nothing had changed.

Hell, maybe I *was* learning to see my life in a more realistic light.

"I've never been brave enough to go on my own," she muttered quietly. "I always thought I'd try it when I had someone to share it with."

"Were you ever lonely traveling all by yourself?" I already knew she was independent, but I'd probably be the first one to admit that *I'd* been pretty damn lonely until I'd discovered what it was like to be with her.

She lifted her head to look at me. "Not always. But sometimes I think I was. I'd rather just have my own company than to be with someone just to avoid being alone, though."

"What about now? Do you *want* to be with me? You were pretty much forced into my company." *Jesus!* I hated the thought of her not being as happy as I was right now.

"Of course I want to be here," she said emphatically. "I don't just share a hammock with *anyone*."

I knew she was teasing, and I grinned back at her.

The woman was a free spirit, and I loved that about her. So I let her get away with not fully answering my question.

Being constantly in the company of another person was new for both of us.

I was used to it already, and I didn't want to change it.

Maybe she was still trying to become accustomed to it.

"Knowing you, I'm surprised you haven't already tried parasailing," I observed. "But I'm kind of glad you haven't. It's something that will be a first for both of us."

Andie was pretty fearless, and she'd done a bunch of terrifying things during her travels.

She rolled out of the hammock before I could stop her. "I'm ready," she pronounced. "Let's do it."

I hated myself for letting her go, but I was drawn to my feet by the pretty flush of excitement on her face.

I wasn't exactly a brave and daring kind of guy. I'd never had a chance to do crazy shit in my life.

Not that parasailing wasn't relatively safe. If it wasn't, I'd be hauling Andie away from danger.

I guess it was just *different* for me to be consenting to something that only a week ago would have made no sense to me.

I didn't do things for *fun*. I did things because it was my *responsibility*.

I pulled on a T-shirt that matched my board shorts.

She pulled on a calf-length coverup over her modest one-piece swimsuit.

My chest hurt as I watched her getting strapped into her seat first. Her gorgeous blonde hair got caught by the wind, and the wayward strands were tossed by the breeze.

Andie was beautiful in a way that I couldn't explain. Conventionally, she *was* pretty, and I shook my head every time she bitched about the extra pounds she carried.

Whether she loved her curves or not, I sure as hell loved them, but it wasn't just her physical appearance that drew me.

It was her spirit, her willingness to accept whatever came her way and turn it into a positive, that really drew me to her.

I was beckoned by a radiance in her that I couldn't even explain, but I didn't try to rationalize the attraction.

It was *there*, and my gut ached every damn time I looked at her.

Mine!

I didn't try to push away my instinctive reactions or my possessiveness when it came to Andie.

Not anymore.

None of it would ever make sense, but it was starting to feel natural, normal, to want to protect Andie, even if she didn't need to be sheltered.

We were shoulder to shoulder as the cable was extended and the parachute picked up the wind.

I wrapped my arm around Andie as we rose, dangling high over the water in a matter of seconds.

She squealed happily, and I let out a bark of rusty laughter as the water stretched out in the distance below us.

"Oh, my God," Andie said loudly. "This is amazing. I feel like I'm flying, Noah."

There *was* a sense of freedom as we hung high above the water, but the weird thing that struck me once we were all the way up was the silence.

I wasn't sure exactly what I'd expected, but it hadn't been the feeling I was actually experiencing as we hung suspended, riding the wind.

"It's a long way down," I said with a grin.

She turned a happy smile my way. "I'm not afraid. We're together."

She leaned into me, and I was completely wrecked.

There was no hesitation in her actions anymore.

She's starting to trust me.

I realized that having Andie's trust meant everything to me. I wanted her to feel completely comfortable when we were together.

"Is this what you expected to be doing on your vacation?" she asked as she laughed from the exhilaration of floating through the sky.

Hell, no, it wasn't.

I hadn't expected to have fun.

I hadn't expected to be amused.

I hadn't expected to learn so much about Mexico.

I hadn't expected to spend every single moment wanting a female so bad that it was almost painful.

I hadn't expected to enjoy the food so damn much.

And I sure as hell hadn't expected . . . *her*.

Maybe in the beginning, I hadn't wanted my world to be upended, and I hadn't wanted my regimented life to be forever changed.

But now . . . I was grateful for all those things I'd never expected or wanted. Especially . . . *her*.

I'd desperately *needed* Andie Lawrence. I just hadn't recognized it in the very beginning of this vacation.

"No," I answered honestly. "None of this is what I thought it would be at all."

"Please don't say you're sorry that it's not a working vacation," she pleaded.

How did I tell her that this whole period of vacation time had been like an awakening of some kind?

How did I tell her that I wouldn't change a *damn thing*?

How did I tell her exactly how much I'd needed her to crash into my life and change it?

In the end, I didn't even answer her question. I didn't say anything at all because I had no idea how to put what I felt into words.

She wrapped an arm around my neck and kissed me.

Andie must have been convinced that I *wasn't* sorry, because she didn't bring the subject up again.

CHAPTER 12

ANDIE

I sighed from my seat at the end of the couch and posted what I'd written that day to my blog.

We only had three more days in Cancún, so I wouldn't be writing anything else until I got back to Citrus Beach. I could write about the last few days here when we got back to California. My article for the travel magazine was well underway, so it wouldn't take a lot of work to finish it up.

Work was going well. I just wished I could be as happy about the progression of my relationship with Noah.

I sensed that he didn't want to push too hard. After all, we'd only had an adult relationship for a total of eleven days.

But I knew what I wanted.

I'd known, probably from the first time I'd laid eyes on him, that I wanted to get him naked, and that need had only grown stronger every moment we were together.

Yeah, maybe I had traveled the world, but I had no idea how to let him know that I was ready to throw caution to the wind.

I was done with the cuddling, kissing, and intimate touches that just made me want him with an ache so deep I could feel him in my bones.

It wasn't that I didn't want to be close to him in every way possible, but cuddling was getting to be akin to torture without the satisfaction of giving in to our carnal urges first.

I shot him a sideways glance as I gently closed my computer.

He was seated on the other side of the couch, his head in his laptop.

I took in a deep breath and let it out slowly. Noah had come a long way in just eleven days. The dark circles under his eyes were gone, and the signs of stress that he'd been wearing on his handsome face were almost nonexistent.

He still hadn't experienced a single headache since the day we'd arrived, and I was relieved that I could finally assume that the frequent pain was actually due to stress.

The relaxed expression on his handsome face looked pretty damn good on him.

Maybe taking this relationship all the way to its obvious conclusion wasn't a good idea. We were only three days away from our departure. But I really didn't want to regret a single moment of this interlude, and I knew I *was* going to be sorry if I let the opportunity to be with Noah intimately just pass me by.

I'd probably never get another shot at it.

I gnawed on my bottom lip for a moment before I finally decided to just blurt it out. "I want to sleep with you, Noah."

Great. Really smooth. I got right into that subject with a lot of tact.

His head jerked up immediately. I didn't have to slam his computer shut anymore to get his attention. "What?"

The poor guy looked confused, and I really couldn't blame him. "I said, 'I want to sleep with you.' Well, maybe not just *sleep.*"

God, I'm really failing miserably at letting him know exactly what I want. Problem is, I have no experience at being a seductress.

I figured my best bet was just to be honest.

Noah cleared his throat. "Andie, are you sure?"

I couldn't look at him because I was so damn embarrassed, but I could feel his gaze burning into my skin.

"Positive. No strings attached, Noah. No promises. I just want to . . . be with you. We only have three more days of this vacation." *And I don't want to end it without experiencing what it would be like to be with you.*

The attraction went both ways. I knew it did, or I wouldn't have brought the subject up.

Really, I was kind of wishing I *hadn't* started the whole conversation. It was awkward.

Maybe I just should have crawled into his lap and started to divest him of his clothing. He'd have gotten the picture without me needing to say a word.

He set his computer on the coffee table, but I never anticipated that my own computer would be falling off my lap and onto the floor as Noah breached the distance between us. A few seconds later, I was underneath his powerful body, my hands in his as he held them over my head.

"What if I *want* strings attached?" he asked, his voice husky and warm.

His face was right above me, and as I met his heated stare, my throat went dry with longing. "There don't need to be any. I just want you, Noah. I probably have since the first time I saw you on the jet. I know what I want."

"Jesus, Andie, I want you, too. You have no idea how much. My dick has been hard since the moment you stole my computer. But we've only been together as adults for eleven days. And I didn't want you to think that my only priority was getting laid." His eyes were so open and honest that my heart tripped.

"I know that," I said softly. "We're having an incredible time together, and we haven't even had sex yet."

"Not because I didn't want it," he growled.

"Then take what you want." I hated the fact that my voice was almost pleading.

His head swooped down, and he captured my lips with a muffled groan.

I shook off his hands and wrapped my arms around his neck, reveling in the sensation of his possession.

The man wasn't tentative or hesitant. When Noah wanted something, he went after it. I was giddy that he was putting his dogged determination toward getting . . . me.

His mouth was hot and hard, and there was no more flirtation or teasing.

Noah meant business, and I was more than happy to meet him with the same ferocious intent.

God, yes!

His hand went behind my head, holding me like he was afraid I was going to move or change my mind.

I threaded my hands into his coarse, thick hair and moaned at the feeling of those strands brushing over the skin of my fingers.

His embrace was urgent and animalistic, so different from the previous kisses we'd shared that I wanted to weep with relief.

I needed this frenzied passion like I needed to breathe.

I craved it with every fiber of my being.

"Andie," he said hoarsely as he lifted his head and feasted on the sensitive skin of my neck.

I wrapped my legs around his waist and pressed against him. I moaned as I felt how hard he was, which created the liquid heat that rushed between my thighs. "Noah. Please."

Closer.

Closer.

I had to get closer to him.

I squealed in surprise as he swung off the couch, picked me up, and carried me to his bedroom.

I missed the feeling of our bodies pressed together almost immediately, and I wanted to weep with frustration.

Pressing my face into his neck, I inhaled his tempting scent, which had become like an aphrodisiac to me.

Noah never smelled like heavy cologne, probably because he didn't use any.

His fragrance was very masculine, very subtle, and completely irresistible.

He lowered me back to my feet beside the bed and turned on the bedside lamp. It wasn't glaring, just a soft glow of illumination.

"You're so damn beautiful, Andie," he muttered as he grabbed the hem of my cotton shirt and pulled it over my head.

I lifted my arms to help him. "I'm not beautiful," I teased. "My ass is way too big."

"Not another word about that," he warned. "I'm crazy about your ass."

I snorted. "You haven't seen me naked yet." Since I wasn't exactly an exhibitionist, I was a little bit nervous about getting naked, but not enough to let that stop me.

Noah unclipped my bra and smoothed it down my arms until it fell to my feet.

"I'm not there yet. But I'm working on it," he answered in a deep, raspy baritone as his large hands cupped my breasts. "Jesus, Andie. You take my breath away."

Electric shocks zinged through my entire body as his thumbs played over my hard nipples.

This is what it's like when two people are hungry for each other. This is how it feels.

He didn't hurry, and my head fell back as he continued to tease the tight peaks.

"Noah," I whimpered. "I need you."

"You have me, baby. You probably have since day one of this vacation."

I shivered as his hand splayed over my belly and slowly moved toward the waistband of my shorts.

Desperate, I started to paw at his shirt. "Take it off," I insisted.

I wanted to be skin-to-skin with this man so badly that I couldn't take another minute of the clothing that was getting in my way.

He barely missed a beat as his shirt came off, but he didn't press our bodies together.

Noah dropped to his knees and started to divest me of my shorts and my panties.

Yes!

I wasn't feeling body conscious, and even if I was, I wanted him too damn much to care at the moment.

There was barely time for me to kick off the garments before he tore back the covers and tumbled both of us onto the bed.

He ended up on top of me, and nothing had ever felt as good as his weight crushing me into the bedding. I sighed as I finally felt his naked skin against mine.

There was some feral desire inside me that wanted to absorb part of him inside myself.

Noah cupped my cheek, his eyes intense as he said, "I want you to know I haven't done this in a very long time. I had one girlfriend in high school, and we managed to stay together for a year or two after my mother died. After that, there was nobody."

"I don't care." I didn't give a damn how experienced he was or wasn't. If anything, the fact that he didn't run around having a quickie or a one-night stand was incredibly enticing.

He'd chosen to be with *me* when he hadn't picked anyone else. That meant something.

He traced my lips with his fingers. "I just thought you should know. I might not last long."

I was perfectly fine with however long it lasted. I'd relish every single touch until it was over.

If. He'd. Just. Do. It.

"I'll make damn sure you're satisfied first," he said roughly as he lifted himself up and started moving his powerful body down.

"What—" He took one of my nipples into his mouth. "Oh, my God."

Suddenly, I couldn't speak, couldn't think. My brain stopped working as I was swept away by sensation.

"Yes." The word sounded like a purr as it came out of my mouth.

Noah nipped at the turgid nipple, and then his tongue washed over it to soothe the small hurt.

I was completely lost as he kept playing with my breasts, moving from one to the other, giving them both plenty of attention.

My head was spinning when he finally went lower, laving the skin of my belly, driving me toward the brink of insanity.

"Please," I begged, not even sure of what I wanted.

I just needed . . . something more.

Finally, he parted my thighs, but he didn't come back over my body.

I jolted as his fingers delicately played lightly over my pussy. "Oh, God," I moaned.

Pleasure ripped through my body as he lowered his head and tasted the sensitive pink flesh between my thighs.

I was really wet, but he lapped at me like he needed the sustenance to keep on living.

I panted, the stimulation of his tongue almost more than I could take. "Please, Noah," I begged.

It was heaven and hell as his tongue finally found my swollen clit and gave me exactly what I needed.

I speared my hands through his hair and held his head against my core.

I didn't want him to move.

I needed . . .

And I needed . . .

God, I really needed . . .

When Noah finally gently nipped the tiny bundle of nerves, and then gave me the pressure of his tongue, I screamed, "Oh-my-God-yes-please-don't-stop."

My body started to shudder as my orgasm came rushing toward me.

It pounded over me with a force I'd never experienced before. "Noah." His name was a hoarse cry, and it was all I could manage.

Noah didn't stop until I had already spiraled down. He prolonged the pleasure until he'd drained me.

But I still ached for him.

"Fuck me," I said insistently. "I need you."

He reared up and tore at the buttons on his jeans. They came off along with his boxer briefs before he covered my body with his.

"Do you have any damn idea how it feels to hear you screaming my name?" He swooped down and captured my lips, leaving me unable to answer his question.

His kiss was sensual and hot, and my desire wound just a little tighter when I tasted myself on his lips.

I wrapped my arms around him, jubilant when I was finally able to run my hands over the heated, silky skin of his back.

There was a dewy layer of perspiration on his skin that told me just how difficult it had been for him to put his own needs aside.

"Fuck! I can't wait any longer, Andie," Noah said throatily.

"Don't wait!" I wanted this man inside me. *Now.* I had to have that connection. I had to feel it.

He entered me in one smooth, hard thrust.

I let out a grunt as he buried himself to his balls.

"What the hell? Andie?" Noah sounded momentarily confused.

The pain started to ease up slowly, and all I could feel was the fullness of Noah deep inside me.

He didn't move, even though I could feel his muscles tensed from holding back.

He panted for a minute before he choked out, "Why in the hell didn't you tell me you were a virgin?"

CHAPTER 13

ANDIE

I could feel him retreating a little bit, both emotionally and physically.

"Don't stop. Please." I was panicked that he might back off. "I want this. I want you."

He *was* my first, but only because he was the first guy I'd ever needed like this. If he backed away, I wasn't sure I could handle that.

He nuzzled against my ear as he answered. "I don't think I can stop. Not unless you really want me to."

I didn't want him to go *anywhere.*

"I'm fine. Please."

"Does it hurt?"

"No," I told him honestly.

There had been a moment of pain, but I was over it. All I felt now was a deep ache for him to finish what he'd just started.

His breath was coming hard and fast, and I felt every exhalation against the side of my face.

I wrapped my legs around his waist, savoring our connection, silently pleading with him to keep going.

Noah pulled himself nearly out, and then he thrust back in with a gentleness I wasn't sure I wanted.

"Fuck me. Don't hold back, Noah." I had to feel his passion. I wanted to wallow in it.

He started a little more-aggressive rhythm, and my hips began to undulate, meeting him every time he plunged into me.

The pace started to get faster, harder, and my body was primed for it. His motions became powerful and smooth, and I felt my body wind even tighter with every thrust.

"Yes. Yes. Yes." I chanted my encouragement, lost in the motion of our bodies in sync.

Noah was relentless as his cock pummeled me over and over.

Harder and harder.

Faster and faster.

Something began unfurling inside me, and all I could do was go along for the ride.

My nails scored Noah's back, and I whimpered as my core clenched around his enormous, rock-hard cock.

My climax hit full force, and I felt like I was being torn into little pieces and tossed into space.

My inner muscles tightened around his cock, as though my body never wanted to let him go.

"Fuck! Andie!" he groaned.

My orgasm milked Noah to his own heated release. His big body shuddered on top of me, and I felt as rocked by the experience as he seemed to be.

He rolled to my side and collapsed, his breath sawing in and out of his lungs as we both tried to recover.

"What in the hell just happened?" he asked hoarsely once we were able to catch our breath.

"We had amazing sex?" I ventured, my voice little more than an anxious squeak.

He rolled onto his side and stared at me. "It was the *only* time you've had sex."

I nodded, feeling resigned to the fact that I was going to have to try to explain. "Yes."

"Why?"

He reached out and stroked my hair. Noah didn't appear to be angry. His expression was more awed than upset.

I rolled on my side to face him. His eyes were filled with questions, and I knew I'd have to answer some of them.

"It's not like I was saving my V-card," I tried to explain. "I don't have some weird idea that I *need* to do that. I just never found somebody I actually wanted to be with."

I'd never wanted to share my body like this, so I . . . hadn't.

"No boyfriend?" he questioned.

"Not really. I dated when I was younger, but nothing serious. But then I started traveling, and I never had a chance to have a real relationship. It just worked out this way. It was no big deal."

"It's a big deal to me, Andie," he rasped. "It's a *really* big deal. Knowing I'm the first guy who has ever been inside you makes me crazy. But your first time should have been different."

"Don't," I said urgently. "Please don't apologize for it. We don't do apologies, remember? And I don't want you to be sorry. I'm not."

His eyes were wild as they met and held mine. "You think I'm sorry?"

I nodded slowly.

"I'm not. Fuck! How could I be?" he asked in an urgent tone. "I'm just a little stunned. I only wish I had known before we were at the point of no return. I would have been more careful. I wouldn't have rushed things."

"I didn't want to go slow," I told him. "I was beyond ready."

"Why me?" he asked gruffly.

I shrugged. "Why not? It's the first time I've ever really wanted to be with someone. I'm not going to get all freaked out over it. I told you, no strings attached. I just wanted to be . . . with you." The last thing I wanted was for him to feel like he owed me anything because he was my first.

"Christ! And I was worried about *my* inexperience," he grumbled. "Why in the hell didn't you tell me?"

Noah sounded hurt, and I hated that. "I was afraid you'd be uptight about it," I explained. "Or that you'd stop. Losing my virginity just isn't a major life event to me."

He shot me a sharp glance. "Taking your innocence was a major life event for me."

I reached out and stroked his rough jawline. "Don't make it that way. All I wanted was to be with you. Being a virgin wasn't something I prized. It's just the way things rolled. No hot guy in my life; no sex."

"You consider me that hot guy?" He gave me a dubious look.

I smiled at him. "The hottest one *I've* ever met. I find you completely irresistible, Noah Sinclair."

He leaned forward and gave me a gentle kiss before he said, "You're crazy."

"You're gorgeous," I shot back at him.

Really, my attraction to Noah wasn't all physical, even though he *was* breathtakingly handsome.

I'd seen plenty of beautiful men, but they'd never made me feel the way Noah did.

There was something else that drew me to him, and I was helpless to explain it. It was honestly inexplicable. He was like a part of me that had been missing before we met.

I craved him like I needed to be connected to him to be whole.

I was telling him the absolute truth when I'd said that I'd never felt this way before, and that I'd never really wanted to be with anyone else.

"It's hard to believe that you didn't hook up with anybody in college," he mused.

I tensed. "I told you that I dropped out to travel."

"But you attended for two years before that."

"Maybe I was just waiting for you," I teased.

Even as I said those words, I had to wonder if there wasn't a lot of truth to them. I'd gone out with a few guys during my first year of college, but the connection had just never been there for me.

They'd been attractive.

They'd been intelligent.

They'd been nice.

But there had been nothing there for me. *Nada. Nothing. Zilch.*

I'd had no desire to get down and dirty with a single one of them.

"You do realize that your opportunity to experiment is over. You're stuck with me," he grumbled.

I laughed. "No strings, remember?"

"I'm about ready to tie you to me with some *very thick rope.* Fuck the strings." He shot me a warning glance. "This wasn't just a fling for me, Andie. I don't do flings. I've wanted to fuck you since day one."

I shivered. Obviously, he'd felt the same chemistry I had when we'd first seen each other again. I wasn't sure why that surprised me. Maybe because he'd hid it so well in the beginning. "I thought you considered me a flake since I dropped out of college to 'flit' around the world."

He shook his head. "If I gave you that impression, I didn't mean it. We've just lived such different lives. I spent most of my adult life taking care of my family, trying to make sure that they were going to be okay. You grew up wealthy."

"And really lonely," I confessed. "The money has never meant that much to me."

"I get that now," he said, his tone full of remorse. "I felt pretty alone, too. I just never admitted that to anyone. I couldn't."

"I think that's where we're a lot alike," I pondered. "It doesn't matter that I was set financially, and you were counting pennies. Neither one of us really had anybody to talk to about how we felt. The only one I had was Owen, and even though he's been the most amazing friend I could ask for, he was surrounded by family who supported *him*. You get what it's like to not really have anybody because you had to be the strongest one, the head of your family."

"I needed them to *think* I was strong," he agreed. "I felt like I needed to keep that facade in place. If I didn't, who could they go to with their problems?"

"But where did *you* go for your strength?"

He grimaced. "I remembered my promise to my mom."

I rolled closer to him, and he spooned me as I said, "That vow was what kept you going."

"Always."

I relished the feel of his powerful body at my back, both of us naked, our skin finally pressed together. I felt protected and cherished as he wrapped an arm around me and pulled me as tightly against him as possible.

I sighed. Being like this with Noah was like . . . coming home for me.

The man was a natural protector, and it was the first time I remembered really feeling . . . safe.

Adored.

Important.

Necessary to someone.

It was a heady and possibly addictive state to be in. But I knew I couldn't get used to the euphoric emotions I was experiencing.

It isn't going to last. We only have a few more days here in Cancún.

Noah might jokingly talk about us being tied together, but it wasn't going to happen. It couldn't.

I can't be tied to anyone, whether I want to be or not.

"I meant it when I said you were done experimenting," he grunted into my ear. "You're mine now, Andie."

I knew I shouldn't feel the shiver of excitement that coursed through my being at his announcement.

It was primal.

Alpha.

Possessive.

And there was absolutely no room for negotiation in his words.

Strangely, that didn't trouble me at all. Well, except for the fact that I couldn't possibly have a future with him. But we had *right now*. I *was* his at the moment.

Honestly, I didn't believe that Noah meant forever, either. It was just an emotional moment for both of us.

"I don't want to be with anybody else," I confessed.

"I think I'd lose my shit if I saw you with anybody else." His arm tightened around my waist.

He'll never see me with anyone else because that can never happen.

"Because I was a virgin?" I questioned.

"Because you're . . . you," he growled. "Because you're supposed to be with me."

"Then you're supposed to be mine, too," I joked.

I was joking, but why was the whole thought of this man belonging to me so damn appealing?

"Already am," he agreed wholeheartedly. "You've got me by the balls, woman. What are you going to do with them?"

I squirmed and turned until I was facing him, and the expression of devotion in his eyes nearly leveled me. My heart started to contract so hard that I could hear every beat of it pounding in my ears.

I can't start thinking about tomorrow. I can't start to believe that Noah is supposed to be my everything.

"I have a lot of time to make up for," I said huskily as I slid my hand down his body and wrapped my fingers around his enormous cock. "It took me way too long to find you."

"Sweetheart, we didn't even talk about birth control, but if you get pregnant—"

"I won't," I interrupted. "I've been on birth control for years to regulate my periods. The last thing you need right now is another child to raise, Noah."

He was barely starting to live his own life. He needed to find himself before he was forced to start giving again.

He needed to be selfish.

He needed to figure out who *he* was before he had to think about a kid.

I searched his face, and I wasn't sure if he was relieved or disappointed that I was protected.

He closed his eyes and groaned as I started to stroke his cock. "You're going to get a lot more than you bargained for if you keep that up," he rumbled ominously. "You'll end up not being able to walk tomorrow."

I snorted. "I think it would be a fair tradeoff."

I knew I was poking the beast, but I didn't care. I wanted more of Noah. I wanted whatever he'd give me for as long as it lasted. I needed to explore him, see what made him lose his mind.

He lifted me over his body, and I was in the perfect position to touch every inch of him until my curiosity was satisfied.

"I hope to hell there's nothing on your itinerary for tomorrow," he growled as I nipped at his earlobe.

"Nothing important," I whispered into his ear.

I'd done everything I needed to in Cancún.

Right now, my priority was the gorgeous, muscular, powerful man underneath me.

"Good. We'll call room service when we get hungry," he said in a graveled tone.

That worked for me.

CHAPTER 14

ANDIE

The following three days were the happiest I'd ever experienced in my entire life.

They were also the most bittersweet days, because I knew that my stolen time with Noah was coming to an end.

We screwed on almost every surface of the hotel suite, but rather than scratching the painful itch he'd caused inside me, it only made me want him more every single time.

Noah was addictive, and it got to the point where he could undo me with a single touch.

A word.

A look.

A wicked laugh.

Then again, I knew I had the same effect on him, and that knowledge was pretty damn powerful.

Three days of doing very little except exploring each other's desires had honed my skills in seduction.

Not that Noah needed all that much encouragement. He seemed almost insatiable.

Seriously, I wasn't about to start complaining about that.

The man had made me drown in pleasure, and be quite happy about the fact that I'd given in to it.

"Do you think the flight attendant was scandalized when I just grabbed the tray of food from her and slammed the door?" Noah drawled, not sounding worried about his actions at all.

Our flight home was way different from our journey to Cancún.

For one, Noah was sprawled out naked on the bed, and I was sitting cross-legged in front of him in one of the white bathrobes provided for the flight.

A moment ago, he'd basically just reached out a hand for the tray of food he'd asked for, hiding his nude body behind the door. He'd closed it the moment he had the food inside the bedroom, without a single word to the flight attendant.

The feast was now between us, and we were both eating like we'd been deprived for days.

"It's Eli's jet," I told him right before I shoved some grapes into my mouth, chewed, and then swallowed. "I doubt that it's anything she hasn't experienced before. I didn't even know this aircraft had a bedroom."

The suite was hidden in the back. It had not only a bedroom but an attached bathroom as well.

He frowned. "Are you trying to say that my little sister has been in here with him?"

I snorted. "Seriously, Noah? I've seen Jade and Eli in town once or twice. They're crazy about each other. Do you really think they *haven't* been in here whenever they fly?"

"The bastard," he said grumpily.

I was fairly certain that Jade participated with gusto, but I didn't mention it. Obviously, the thought of his sister being with a guy was an unsavory thing for Noah to talk about. "They are married," I pointed out.

"Doesn't matter," he said roughly. "She's my baby sister."

I laughed. "But you aren't upset that this jet has a bedroom right now."

He shot me a mischievous grin. "Not at all."

We'd already made use of the room a couple of times since he'd hauled me back here. "So stop complaining."

"Baby, I'm not complaining about anything right now." His voice was low and contained a note of warning that sent a shiver of pleasure down my spine.

"Food." I pointed at the half-empty tray.

We hadn't come up for air very often during the last couple of days, so we were both starving.

He nodded. "Eat."

I swallowed a bite of the sandwich I'd just started to devour. It made my heart ache every time I saw how nothing was more important to Noah than *me* having *my* needs met.

I had to wonder how many times Noah had sacrificed his own food for one of his brothers or sisters when they were younger.

He was like that. Noah would have let me eat the entire tray if he thought it would help me, and not touch a bite himself, even if he was hungry.

That was just the kind of guy Noah was. He sacrificed, and never thought it was something out of the ordinary.

I just hoped, when Noah found his forever woman, that she'd realize that about him, and make sure that he didn't sacrifice his own needs too much.

"I'm done," I told him. "I can't eat another bite. Go for it."

"You sure?" His eyes were doubtful. "We missed breakfast this morning."

119

Skipping that meal hadn't exactly been difficult, considering I'd been busy having one of the most extraordinary orgasms I'd ever experienced.

"Seriously. I'm stuffed." I rubbed my stomach.

I smiled as I watched Noah tear into the rest of the food.

The man could definitely eat, and it made me happy just to watch him do it. I knew that Noah had never stopped to actually *enjoy* food, so I'd loved every moment of the trip when I could watch him try something different.

He wasn't picky.

He was willing to try almost anything, provided it wasn't alive and moving.

Noah set the empty tray aside on the small table next to the bed and reached for me. I collapsed at his side and put my head on his shoulder as he pulled me close.

I want to enjoy these last moments with him. Tuck them away inside my heart.

"I think I need to get my own jet," he said thoughtfully. "I'd like to do some traveling."

My heart skipped a beat. "You would? Where would you go?"

I didn't want to get my hopes up that he might be willing to take a bunch of time off to make up for all of the years he'd spent every moment of his day taking care of others and working.

I wanted that for him, but that was something he needed to decide for himself.

"Australia." His tone was introspective. "Europe. Africa." He took a deep breath. "Hell, I've never seen anything other than Southern California."

"I've never been to Australia or Africa. Not yet."

"We'll go together. Andie, I know we haven't talked much about the future."

"Let's not," I said hastily. "Let's just focus on today."

Please, don't. I want to enjoy these last few hours.

"You don't understand. I *want* to talk about it." He sat up, taking me with him until we were face to face, his hands on my shoulders. "I want to plan things together. You're the one who pulled me out of myself, made me want to finally have a life of my own. I want *you* with *me*."

"Maybe we could plan a trip," I said carefully.

I could do that, right? I took this one. One more wouldn't hurt.

I wanted what Noah was offering with every ounce of my being, and my heart was bleeding because there were some things I just *couldn't* offer him.

He shook me gently. "I want to do more than just plan a damn trip. When we get home, I want to do some real *dates*. I want to spoil you rotten because you're my woman. Eventually, I want to propose marriage to you, and have you say *yes*. I know I'm going to have to earn that right. But I don't give a shit. Someday, you *are* going to be my wife, Andie, because fuck knows that I don't even want to imagine not having you with me for the rest of my life."

I cringed, and moved back a little like I'd just seen a poisonous snake. My eyes suddenly filled with tears, and I tried to blink them away. "I don't roll like that, Noah. I'm mindful. I like to live life from moment to moment, day to day. I don't think of the distant future."

Oh, dear God. I hadn't meant to lead him to believe all of this could last forever. Not that I didn't yearn for what he was talking about, but it wasn't the life . . . for me.

"Fuck! Then we can slow it down. You're still young. Maybe you're not ready for marriage. We can date, but I can't deal with you dating anybody else. I'll talk you into taking me on forever someday." The determined look on his handsome face caused a tear to plop onto my cheek, unchecked.

Then another . . .

And yet another . . .

"You can't change who I am, Noah," I said tearfully.

"I don't want to change you," he rasped. "I just want to know that somewhere in the future, I have a damn chance."

I didn't even try to stop the tears from falling. I hadn't cried in years, and now the droplets were leaking out of my eyes like an endless stream.

The pain in my chest was so acute that I felt like my heart was going to explode.

I hurt.

I hurt so damn much.

I would have given anything to have the power to throw myself into his arms and tell him the truth: that there would never be another man in my life like him.

Sometime during the last few weeks, Noah had started to become my everything.

My joy.

My pain.

My pleasure.

My heart.

But I couldn't lie to him. "I can't promise you forever, Noah. It's not me."

He threw his arms out. "So what in the hell was all of this? Some kind of game?"

I shook my head vehemently. "No. Never. When Owen asked me to go with you to Cancún, I really wanted to see you again. Whether you know it or not, you helped when I was a kid. I idolized you. You always seemed to have all of the answers when I didn't. I wasn't a confident child, but you didn't make me feel like I was different because of that. You made me feel some sense of normal. You, and all of your family whenever I was with you."

"So Owen had to talk you into this whole thing," he said harshly. "You weren't going just because you wanted to do some travel writing."

"He broached the opportunity," I said truthfully. "I took him up on it. He didn't have to talk me into it. I'm not going to bullshit you,

Noah. Your family is worried about you. I promised Owen I'd do my best to make you relax. Everything else that happened was all about us."

"According to you, there is no *us*," he said angrily.

I swiped a hand across my face to wipe away the tears, but they just kept falling. "I didn't say that. I *want* to be with you."

He glared at me, and it made me flinch. I wasn't used to seeing the colder side of Noah Sinclair.

"Why? What's the point, Andie, if it's just going to end up with you taking off somewhere and leaving me at the end? Do you really think I'm a damn masochist?" He was really furious. I could tell by his stony expression and the ticking in his stiff jawline.

What's the point?

God, maybe he was right. What *was* the point?

I'd been on the verge of pouring my guts out to him to make him understand why I lived my life this way, but his outburst had stopped me in my tracks.

"There is no point," I conceded as I got up and gathered my clothing from the floor. "I'm sorry."

The pain of walking away from him was excruciating, but I knew it was the right thing to do.

Someone like me wasn't good for him.

He deserved forever.

He deserved total commitment.

He deserved a woman who could give him that, and that female wasn't me.

I went into the bathroom, and then closed and locked the door behind me.

I waited until I got into the shower before I lost all control. I sat on a small stool as the warm water washed over me, and sobbed out the pain and loss that was pummeling me relentlessly.

By the time I was dressed and I'd pulled myself together, we were getting ready to land.

CHAPTER 15

NOAH

"What in the hell is wrong with you, Noah?" my brother Seth questioned a week later as he and Aiden sat at my kitchen table, both of them downing a beer with me. "You came back from Cancún looking better, and a week later, you look like hell again."

At the moment, I would have preferred a big bottle of tequila to the beer I was guzzling, but I made do with the brew from the case that Aiden had brought with him.

"That was vacation," I said stoically. "This is real life."

Honestly, I *had* finished my dating app, and it was in the testing phase. But I hadn't immediately started another project. I'd tried, but I wasn't concentrating well enough to do the start-up work.

"Yeah, well, real life doesn't have to suck," Seth said grimly.

"It does," I told him right before I knocked down a good portion of my third bottle of beer.

"Have you talked to Andie at all?" Aiden asked. "You seemed to be having a good time with her in Cancún."

I'd connected with both Aiden and Seth a few times while I was out of the country, and I hated myself for sounding so enthusiastic at that time. "Not at all," I replied flatly. "Why would I? We had a good time while it lasted, but she's *Owen's* friend."

I tried like hell not to think about that last hour on Eli's jet. It had been awkward and silent. We hadn't said a single word to each other. Not even as we'd disembarked from the jet.

"I got the sense that she might have been a little more than a friend," Aiden pressed.

"A fling," I said, the words tasting bad in my mouth.

Like I'd told Andie, I didn't do flings. But maybe I should think about it in the future. Perhaps it would help me become more sophisticated about screwing a woman and just walking away after our bodies were sated.

I finished my beer and reached for another, pissed off at myself for not just getting over Andie Lawrence.

Problem was, I couldn't forget all of the things that had happened. They played through my mind in a loop, and I watched that particular movie in my head over and over.

Why didn't I see that she wasn't up for more? Why did I think she'd *want* to spend her life with me?

Hell, the entire relationship had been too much, too fast.

Once I'd had a chance to cool down from the anger-that-was-really-pain that I'd experienced after she'd blown me off, I'd done my best to reason things out. I wanted to figure out exactly when our intentions became so *different*.

I'd wanted everything almost from the very beginning.

She'd never said she wanted the same thing.

No strings attached . . .

She'd never taken that back. I'd just assumed that she'd felt differently by the end of the trip.

Dammit! I'd felt her emotions, and she sure as hell should have been able to decipher mine.

I'd chalked the whole thing up to me and Andie just being too . . . different.

I'd wanted *it all.*

She'd wanted nothing except the *experience* of being with me.

I looked up, and two sets of eyes were staring at me inquisitively. Obviously, Aiden and Seth expected me to say more. But I had nothing more to say. I really didn't want them to know I'd fallen hard over a span of two weeks for a woman who wanted no future with me.

I *felt* like a fucking idiot.

I didn't really want to *show* them just how naive I'd been.

Damn both of my brothers for being the type of guys who looked a whole lot deeper than most men did. When it came to family issues, they were relentless.

However, they'd never pushed me about a female or my feelings about one, and I didn't want that to start now. I was the oldest. I was supposed to be giving *them* advice. I didn't need them to try to get me to spill my guts. I didn't do that. Ever.

"What happened?" Seth asked curiously.

My gut hurt with the need to tell them everything so we could try to figure it out together. I wanted to tell someone. *Fuck!* I was sick and tired of trying to keep everything to myself.

Now that I didn't need to be a father figure to my brothers and sisters, I wanted to be their damn brother again.

I *wanted* Seth's and Aiden's advice. After all, they were both married and happy. I *knew* they had more experience with females than I did. Hell, almost *any other man* in the world had more knowledge of women than I did.

It was just so damn hard to shed the instinct to be the oldest and wisest, be that guy who didn't need *anyone*'s input on life situations.

"Nothing happened. We saw a lot of stuff in Mexico. We ate a lot. We fucked. And then it was over." It wasn't exactly a lie, but it wasn't entirely true, either.

"Bullshit, Noah," Aiden said harshly. "You look like your whole damn world is ending, and that's your fourth beer. You rarely have more than one, and *never* more than two. Something's up."

"I'm thirsty," I said as I glared at him.

"Are you working your ass into the ground again?" Seth asked as he surveyed my face.

"No. I can't fucking concentrate," I admitted in an ornery tone.

"Something happened between you and Andie," Aiden stated with no uncertainty.

I glared at him. "Do you think you're psychic now or something?"

"I know *you*, brother," Aiden shot back, sounding unperturbed. "When have you *not* been able to concentrate? When have you just screwed a woman you didn't care about? What the fuck happened?"

I was starting to feel the effects of the alcohol. I'd downed those brews pretty fast, and I really wasn't used to drinking more than one beer in one sitting. "Fine. I wanted more. Andie didn't."

"How much more?" Seth questioned.

I *was* spilling my guts, but damned if I really cared anymore. I needed to get used to the fact that I was now on equal ground with all of my family, that we could just talk like brothers. "I wanted to marry her. Are you happy now?"

Seth let out a low whistle. "Whoa. *That* happened in two weeks?"

"How long did it take you to decide you wanted Riley?"

"Point taken," he replied. "But maybe it happened too fast for Andie. Maybe you scared her away."

I gave up trying to stay mum about what had happened in Cancún. Hell, it was eating me alive. "It's not that," I admitted. "We're just two different people. She likes to frolic around the world without complications in her life. She said she's the type of woman who likes to take one day at a time. And I'm a planner."

Aiden frowned. "Maybe you could have slowed things down."

"Tried that. Offered to do it," I informed him. "Didn't work. She said she could *never* give me forever, so we decided there was no point to the whole relationship. I mean, why would I want to spend more time with her if there was no chance at a future with her at the end?"

"You fell in love with her," Seth stated. "That sucks."

"Of course I fell in love with her," I responded irritably. "I wouldn't have been thinking about marriage if I hadn't."

"What did you like about her if she's a flake?" Aiden asked.

I downed the last of my beer and slammed it on the wooden table. "That's just it. It's not that she doesn't care about *anything*. Actually, she cares about *everything*. Well, everything except *me*." I thought for a moment before I corrected myself. "That's probably not fair. I think she did care about me, just not enough to share her future with me. Andie is . . . a free spirit. She *does* get totally into the moment. What did I like about her? The question should be what *didn't* I like. I liked too damn much about her. The way she laughs. The way she moves. The way she isn't afraid to outeat a man who should be able to put away a lot more food than she can. The way she connects with people, and her empathy. The way she never really wants to hurt anyone. But she did. She just about killed *me*. But it wasn't like she was *trying* to do it. I don't think she has a malicious bone in her body."

"There has to be something more to her statement, then," Seth said thoughtfully. "Some kind of misunderstanding."

"I think so, too," Aiden commented. "I've only run into her once since she's been back, when she was out in town with Owen. But I can tell he adores her. I can't see him having a friend who wasn't real."

"Oh, she's real," I muttered. "She just isn't in love with . . . *me*."

Dammit! I hated saying those words because it still made my gut ache.

"I think you should talk to her," Aiden suggested.

"He can't," Seth injected. "Not in person. She's in Boston with Owen. I spoke to him a couple of days ago, and he was getting ready to leave to go with her."

I jerked my head up. "She's gone? With Owen?"

Christ! Why was I feeling . . . betrayed in some way? After all, Owen had been Andie's friend for a very long time. Wasn't it normal for them to go somewhere together?

I refused to be jealous of my own little brother because he was spending time with Andie and I . . . wasn't.

"Owen decided to take a couple more weeks off before he starts at the clinic. The paperwork was held up, and he said he wanted to have more time to catch up on life. Whatever that means," Aiden remarked.

"It means that he wants to do something other than medicine for a while," Seth informed us. "He bought himself an e-reader, and he said he wanted to do some pleasure reading that didn't involve anything medical. Catch up on the current TV shows. He's lived and breathed becoming a doctor for a decade. He's feeling a little burned out and out of touch."

I nodded. "Understandable." I felt the same way. It was like I'd woken up from a fog and realized there was a world outside of work. No doubt my little brother felt the same way after the intensity of med school and his residency.

"Maybe I should just get a damn e-reader. Right now, I'm jealous of my own brother," I confessed.

"You don't really think Andie and Owen are an item, do you?" Seth asked.

I thought for a minute. *Nope.* I probably *didn't* believe that. Andie had been a damn virgin. If she had anything going with Owen, he was pretty damn slow to act on that. Besides, he'd already told me that he and Andie weren't romantic. "Probably not. He's been her best friend for years, and there's never been a romantic connection. But him being with her right now bugs the hell out of me."

Aiden laughed. "I get it. I really do. I'm starting to think all Sinclair men are possessive bastards."

"But Owen is our brother," Seth proclaimed.

I shot him a dirty look. "Imagine Riley going away with one of us, just as a friend, when she wasn't willing to give *you* the time of day."

"Not happening," he said with a troubled expression. "I get the picture."

I shook my head. "The problem is, I don't have the right to her time, or her attention. We ended it before it got too complicated."

"Why do I have a feeling it's *already* complicated?" Aiden observed. "I think you should talk to her when she comes back, Noah. All of this could be a misunderstanding. Do you really want to give her up *that* easily?"

I slammed my fist down hard on the table, making both of my brothers jump. "Fuck! I didn't want to give her up *at all*. But it's impossible to make somebody care about me the same way I care about them. I'm *not* going to talk to her again. It's pointless."

My brothers exchanged a look, and I knew that they both thought I'd lost it.

I didn't get angry.

I didn't get upset.

I didn't lose it over a female.

Hell, I hadn't really had a woman in my life for way over a decade.

Truth was, I didn't *have* Andie, either. "It was a really pleasant two weeks. Andie did a lot of good things for me during that period of time. Now, let's drop it. I just need to get the fuck over it."

"If you need a distraction, Seth and I are on our way to the docks to see one of my new vessels," Aiden said. "Do you want to come with us? We thought we'd throw some burgers on the grill at my place afterward."

I opened my mouth automatically to say *no*, and then I closed it.

For years, I'd denied myself the company of my brothers unless I *had* to be around.

If I wanted to be honest with myself, I'd missed them.

I didn't want to hang out with them *only* when I felt obligated to be there. I didn't have to do that anymore.

It was time for my relationships to change with all of my siblings. Maybe I'd never get over the instinct to dole out advice and keep them safe, but I could start doing that as a big brother instead of a parent figure, right?

"Yeah, I think I'd like that. If you don't mind, I'll stop by for some food at your place, too." I looked at Aiden. "I think Mexico gave me a taste for more than a cold sandwich."

Aiden nodded. "Maya's been asking about you. We'll all be glad to have you there."

"You'll have to fill me in on the commercial-fishing business and what you're doing. I'd like to catch up on both of your lives."

My brothers looked stunned, and I watched as they tried pathetically to hide that shock.

Jesus! Had I really been *that* bad? Had I distanced myself so much that they were surprised that I actually wanted some details?

The short answer was probably *yes*, and I hated myself for not being a more active part of their lives after they'd grown up. I'd been there when they'd actually come to me, but I hadn't exactly reached out the way a big brother should.

I added, "I could use a little advice on my portfolio, and some information about buying myself a jet of my own. Eventually, I might decide to do some traveling. And I'd really like to take as much work off Evan as I possibly can."

Maybe I wouldn't be traveling with Andie, but I was starting to appreciate the value of getting away and experiencing other parts of the world.

"You're actually going to spend some of your money?" Seth asked, sounding surprised.

I shrugged. "I have a shitload of it, right?"

Aiden grinned. "We all do."

"I think I'm just starting to realize that I'm filthy rich," I confessed. "It's taken some time for me to see it as real instead of a fantasy."

"Oh, it's real. And we'll be more than happy to help you spend some of that money," Seth said with a grin.

I looked from one of my brothers to the other, realizing just how much I'd missed by not being there with them, especially after we'd received the money and had no reason not to work things out in our heads *together*. "I want to be a better man, and a better . . . brother. I might need your help." My voice was hoarse with emotion.

Their expressions were deadly serious as Seth said, "Noah, you're one of the best men I know. I wouldn't change you."

Aiden nodded his agreement.

I swallowed the lump in my throat. Obviously, my siblings were going to easily forgive the mistakes I'd made in my life. "When Mom died, I promised that I'd keep my head down, work, and make sure you're all okay. I guess I never saw the signal when that should have ended and I should have become a brother again."

"Because that's who you are, Noah," Seth said quietly as he and Aiden both stood. "You give, and give, and give, without hesitation. There was never a pause, so obviously you *couldn't* see it. Do you think any of us are ever going to criticize because you cared too damn much, or were so single-minded about making sure that we were okay? No. We aren't. We just want you to let us care about you now, too. You don't have to take every one of our problems onto your shoulders anymore. Hell, we don't have any problems, really. We're filthy rich and happy."

"Then help *me* think like a rich guy, and catch me up on reality," I requested.

"We can do that. It's the least we can do," Aiden agreed as he slapped me on the back. "It's going to be good to have you as a brother again, Noah."

For some reason, I felt like a ton of bricks had been lifted off my shoulders.

Maybe because I realized that I didn't have to be the head of the family anymore.

I didn't have to have all the answers.

I didn't have to make sure everyone was happy.

I didn't have to push my own feelings aside to take care of everyone else.

I didn't have to solve everyone's problems.

All I had to do anymore was to be a good brother to all of my siblings, and let them care about me like a brother instead of some kind of parent figure.

Maybe the instinct to act like their father was always going to be there, but I could control it. No doubt it would get easier as time went by.

It was time for me to take up a new role in my extraordinary family, and I was beyond relieved and excited about that.

CHAPTER 16

ANDIE

"Hello. Earth to Andie. Can you hear me?"

I lifted my head and stared at Owen, realizing he'd been talking but I hadn't heard a single word he'd said.

"Sorry," I mumbled. "Can you repeat that?"

He gave me an exasperated look from his seat across from me in the small Boston bistro. "What's wrong? You're always present in a conversation. But you look lost today. Is it because of what happened earlier? Everything is okay, Andie, just in case you missed the good news."

I nodded, feeling guilty. "I know. I'm happy. I guess I was just thinking about an article I need to write."

Lying to Owen made me feel even worse, but how could I tell him that I was distracted because I couldn't stop thinking about his older brother and the devastation I'd seen on Noah's face as we'd parted ways a week ago?

Owen and I had managed to have a decent time in Boston. I'd asked him to come to this restaurant so I could review the place for my blog. He certainly hadn't argued. Now that he was wealthy, Owen acted like he was making up for lost opportunities by visiting every restaurant in sight.

"Something's eating at you. You haven't said much about what happened in Cancún. I haven't seen Noah since the day he got back, but he looked better, and he definitely gained a few pounds. Did you have a good time?" he questioned.

I nearly choked on my dessert.

"We . . . did," I answered cautiously. "Noah was pretty open minded, and we had a chance to do a lot of different things there. I'm pretty sure he enjoyed most of them."

Noah had certainly liked making me climax until I was mindlessly chanting his name.

He'd also enjoyed licking tequila from my breasts, but probably not quite as much as I had.

And he'd really seemed to appreciate it when I'd tried to swallow his entire cock whole.

My technique might have been lacking due to my inexperience, but I knew he'd enjoyed it anyway.

In fact, he'd been downright elated.

"Good food?" Owen inquired.

"The best," I retorted shortly.

"Come on, Andie. What are you *not* saying? Talk to me."

I put my fork on my empty dessert plate and pushed it away. "I don't know what you mean."

"We've been friends since you decided to paint my entire face with watercolors when we were in the third grade. You know exactly what I mean. Since when have you held back anything from me?" Owen sounded hurt.

Hmmm . . . maybe since I fucked your older brother?

Yeah. No. I'm not about to say that out loud.

Owen *was* my best friend, the person I generally confided in, but I couldn't just blurt out what had happened in Cancún. With his older *brother*.

"It's been a stressful couple of days," I told him. "I'm just a little distracted."

He shook his head. "Nope. It's not that."

Damn! I hated it that Owen knew me so well.

Obviously, Noah hadn't shared much about our trip to Cancún, but Owen usually knew when something was bothering me. "Let's just say that maybe Noah and I got a little too close, and leave it at that."

He leaned back in his chair. "Oh, hell no. I'm not about to let you get away with that. What happened?"

I shot him a desperate look. "I really care about him, Owen. And I think I hurt him. I didn't mean to do it."

He leaned forward and grabbed my hand. "Andie, if that happened, I *know* you didn't mean to do it. I haven't seen much of Noah, but he didn't say anything about that."

I probably shouldn't have said anything, either. But I felt like I was dying inside, and Owen was my best friend. "We decided not to see each other anymore."

He raised a brow. "Why?"

"He said he wanted to marry me someday. You know I don't do forever. I can't."

Owen smirked. "Holy shit! You two *are* perfect for each other. I knew it. Noah needs somebody like you, Andie."

I pushed his hand away. "Didn't you hear me? He was talking about the possibility of getting *married* in the future."

He frowned. "So, marry him once you've done the whole official dating thing. Or, hell, just marry him without dating. Who the fuck cares? Or didn't you fall for him, too?" Owen sounded troubled now.

"I did," I admitted wistfully. "Hard."

"So what's the problem?"

"*I'm* the problem. You know my philosophy, and why I operate that way. No forever. No long-term planning. He's your brother, Owen. You, of all people, have to understand why I don't want to start a serious relationship."

"Andie," Owen said in a soothing voice. "The entire situation is different now. That was five years ago. Did you tell him everything? I know my brother. He'd understand."

"I wanted to," I explained. "But when he started talking about forever, I choked."

"Do you feel like you might want forever with him?"

My eyes filled with tears. "I would. I do. That's not the point. It doesn't matter what I *want*. You know that. It wouldn't be fair to Noah to offer him something that wasn't mine to give."

"That's crap, Andie. That's Noah's decision to make. You should have told him everything. I get why you were reluctant before, but it's been five years, Andie."

The tears escaped and started to flow down my cheeks. "I don't know if I can take that chance."

"You won't know unless you try. Christ, Andie! You and Noah both deserve better than the hand you were dealt in life. I wanted you two to be together in Cancún because you both deserve to be happy. Noah's too damn serious. I can't even remember the last time he actually smiled. I knew you could show him how to live in the moment. To enjoy the opportunities that are out there. I think Noah's good for you, too. He's as solid as a rock. If he cares about you, he's always going to be there."

"I-I know that," I choked out. "I just don't know if I can be there for *him* the same way. It wouldn't be fair if I couldn't."

"Life sucks. It's seldom fair," he said drily. "If there's one thing you've taught me, it's to reach for every bit of happiness I can find."

I took a deep breath, let it out, and swiped the tears from my face. "The relationship was getting out of control. Everything happened so fast."

He grinned. "Since when do you shy away from something hard or difficult to understand?"

"Since I met your brother," I replied wryly. "You're right about Noah. He's the type of guy who would always be there. Maybe that's what fascinated me about him in the beginning. He tossed his entire life aside to be there for his family. That takes . . . somebody special."

"That's Noah," he agreed. "But you're special, too, Andie. Don't walk away if you don't want to. You don't have to do that anymore. I know you only live for today, but don't make the mistake of letting yourself get buried in the past so deep that you're passing something by that's worth hanging on to now."

"It isn't that he isn't worth it," I argued.

"Think about it, Andie," he answered harshly. "What's Noah going to think? With no explanation at all from you, he's going to assume that he wasn't worthy. Or that you didn't feel that he was. Is that fair to him? At this point in his life, does he really need that kind of blow to his self-worth? He obviously cared, and you just walked away without a word. He's been left to make his own assumptions, and Noah is pretty good at blaming himself."

"I don't want him to do that. It's me. Not him."

"Then I think you should tell him that," Owen snapped. "At least he won't think it's him, and that he fucked up."

I went to pick up the check, but Owen snatched it away. "Oh, no you don't. I never thought I'd say this, but I'm more loaded than you are. I'm buying."

I scowled at him. "It's a business lunch."

"Tough," he answered as he pulled a bunch of bills from his wallet and dropped them on top of the check. "Let's get going. We have a bracelet to pick up."

I smiled weakly. "We do, right?"

The waiter came by and picked up the check. Owen told him to keep the change as we were walking out the door.

The jewelry store was just a few doors down, so we walked to it.

"I think you're right," I said softly as we walked side by side. "Noah has the right to know. I gave that to him when we got . . . intimate. I still don't think I can do forever, but I should have just told him about my past."

Owen smirked as he held the door of the jewelry store open for me. "Do you think for one single second that my stubborn older brother isn't going to give you the fight of your life once you tell him? Noah isn't exactly a man-whore. If he slept with you, and started talking marriage, he's crazy about you. My big brother would take that kind of shit pretty seriously."

I stepped into the small store, and the owner waved. "I'll get your order," she called happily before she disappeared into the back.

"Then maybe telling him is a mistake." I wasn't sure I could fight Noah when he was determined. "He is pretty bullheaded when he wants to be."

Honestly, I didn't want to fight Noah at all.

I wanted to get him naked and find the same bliss that we had in Cancún.

I wanted to tell him that I wanted to marry him, even though I couldn't.

I wanted to tell him that I was ready to talk about our future, even though I wasn't.

To be truthful, I was . . . terrified.

Owen took my arm and led me up to the counter. "No fear, Andie."

I looked up at him and smiled. It had been our mantra since we were younger. It had gotten us in trouble more than a few times. "I don't think that's going to work this time," I said, my tone melancholy.

"Of course it will. Now tell me about your sex life with Noah. Was he a stud?" he asked jokingly.

I raised my chin. "Like I'm going to tell you *that*? Butt out of that business, mister."

I knew Owen, and I got that he was letting me make this particular decision on my own, now that he'd had his say.

He'd be there for me if I needed him, but he was letting me settle things in my own mind and in my own way.

I sighed before I said, "I'll tell him. But no other promises."

He grinned. "Then I'm not worried. I know my brother. If he's crazy about you, he's not going anywhere, and he's sure as hell not going to let you walk away without a fight."

Maybe *that* was why I was really afraid. Nobody had ever stuck with me except Owen, not even my own parents. Generally, people floated through my life, but never became . . . attached.

Deep down, I desperately wanted to feel that attachment, even though, at the same time, I'd spurned it.

"Here we go," the owner said as she breezed out from the back room. "It's all done, and it's beautiful."

She took the delicate bangle bracelet out of the box and handed it to me. My hand shook a little as I took it.

"This is it, Andie," Owen said solemnly. "Number five."

I held my arm up and surveyed the other four bracelets around my wrist. They were all thin, just enough of a circle to be able to number them.

Number one was white gold.

Number two was rose gold.

Number three was yellow gold.

Number four was a combination of all of the colors twisted into one bracelet.

I surveyed the one I was buying today. This one was platinum because it was special.

The jeweler had engraved it with a single word.

Five.

I pushed the delicate circle over my hand and onto my wrist with a tremulous breath.

"Done," I said to Owen softly.

"Thank God!" he exclaimed in a deep baritone before he wrapped his arm around my shoulders.

I threw myself into his arms and basked in the comfort of his rough hug.

"Everything is going to be fine, Andie," he said in a husky voice beside my ear.

He said that *every* time I got a new bracelet.

But this time, I almost believed him.

CHAPTER 17

ANDIE

I went to see Noah the day after I returned from Boston, and I nearly turned around and left the moment I pulled into his driveway.

What's the point of telling him about my past? It isn't like it's going to change anything.

I stopped my sporty convertible in front of his garage and turned off the engine.

It doesn't matter whether it changes anything. It doesn't have to change anything. It's all about Noah and his perception of what happened the day we decided to end it.

I was going to tell him because I should have done it before we'd ever gotten intimately involved.

I'd just never expected him to say that he wanted to stay with me.

That he wanted to date me.

That he was going to want marriage in the future.

I took a deep breath and let it out as I put my keys in my purse.

Coward!

I wasn't going to run away again. I wasn't going to let all of this go without him knowing everything.

Even if I *hadn't* hurt him, I'd thought about what might have gone on in his mind, and I hadn't liked the direction those conclusions had headed.

What if he thought he was being rejected? He didn't know that the issues between us were not about him and all about . . . *me.*

If nothing else, I might have damaged his ego, and that was the last thing I'd intended.

Noah had just started to join the world again.

I didn't want him to feel let down before he'd completely found his way.

That was why I was here to tell him the truth. If he knew, he'd never doubt that the problem was me and not him.

The man was so incredibly lovable that I didn't want him to think, for even a moment, that he wasn't.

I'll tell him, and we can both move on.

My bracelets jingled as I adjusted my purse across my body, the sound a reminder of just how far I'd come from where I'd been years ago.

I didn't ever want to go back. Really, I didn't even want to talk about what had happened, which was why I avoided thinking about the darker times in my life.

Just do it!

Determined, I shoved my arm against the car door and got out. I stopped in my tracks as I closed it.

His house is amazing.

The home was really big, but I couldn't say it was ostentatious. It was beautifully landscaped, and the lawn was well manicured. However, it stopped just short of being simply another mansion on the water.

It was an older home, but it was charming, with stonework in the front that reminded me of rocks that you could find on the beach.

There were a couple of palm trees and some well-placed, colorful plants that kept the house from being too stodgy and uniform.

I smiled as I approached the front door and noticed that it was a deep burgundy shade, which was a nice pop of color to keep the washed-out rock from being boring and bland.

If a big, rambling house could be charming, Noah's home was exactly that. Just like my adorable little cottage, the place felt homey rather than showy.

I pushed the doorbell, hoping like hell that Noah was home. I wasn't sure I could bring myself to keep coming back.

There were several garages, so I definitely couldn't identify his absence simply by noting there was no car in the driveway.

I startled at the sound of the door opening. It was Noah, and my eyes were immediately drawn to his face.

My heart melted just from seeing him again, even as I looked at his exhausted, wary face.

He looked tired and defeated, a look I'd never seen on him before, and I didn't like it.

The thought that I might have put that kind of expression on his handsome face made my heart sink.

"Can we . . . talk?" I asked hesitantly.

"Why?" he asked brusquely. "I thought we'd already said everything there was to say."

"I didn't," I said simply.

He swung the door open without a word and walked away.

I closed the door behind me and followed him.

Okay, maybe it wasn't the warmest welcome, but at least he'd let me in.

I found him in the kitchen, making himself some coffee. "Can I have one of those?" I asked.

I was dragging ass. It was my first day back in Citrus Beach, and even though it was only a three-hour time difference from Boston, I hadn't slept well.

He pulled his mug from the single-cup coffeemaker. "Help your-self," he said gruffly as he leaned against the kitchen cupboard and took a sip of the steaming brew.

I opened the cupboard over the coffeemaker, and got lucky on the first try when I found a mug. I rifled around in the drawer with the coffee pods, found one that sounded strong, popped it into the appropriate slot, and shoved the mug underneath.

"I won't take up much of your time. I'll try to be quick," I said nervously as I waited for the coffee.

"Why are you here, Andie?" he said curtly. "You already said you don't do forever, and you were pretty clear about where you stood on the flight back."

I made myself at home and found the cream and sugar to add to my coffee. I was pretty sure he wasn't going to offer to get them himself.

I took a sip of the doctored coffee before I answered. "It's not that I *don't* do forever, Noah. It's that I *can't* do it."

"I don't follow you," he said impatiently.

"Can we sit?" I didn't want to explain while I was standing in the middle of his kitchen.

He jerked his head toward the right, and I trailed behind him, sipping on my coffee in the hope that it might give me some energy, until we got to what looked like a family room.

I sank into a nice, cushy leather recliner. It was comfortable, but it didn't help me feel less uptight.

"So I guess you're back from your trip to Boston with Owen," he stated flatly.

"Yeah. I didn't know you were keeping tabs on me."

"I wasn't. Owen is part of my family, remember? We all keep tabs on each other."

I hated myself for feeling a little disappointed that he sounded more worried about his brother than he was about me. In some stupid, ridiculous way, I wanted him to be concerned about me, which made absolutely no sense in my rational mind.

"I guess I wouldn't know that because I don't really have any family. Nobody has ever really cared where I go and what I do," I said honestly. "And yes, we're obviously back."

God, I hated the awkwardness between me and Noah. It had never been that way before that last hour or two on our flight back from Cancún.

I hated it.

The tension in the room was nearly unbearable.

I needed to get on with what I came for and get the hell away from Noah.

My heart was shattered, and I was going to need time to try to put it back together again.

Whatever Noah and I had shared, it was gone. There was no point in tormenting myself.

I couldn't see a single sign of any emotion on Noah's stony face, and I hated that, too. He'd openly expressed himself on the trip, smiled readily, and let me know when he was feeling any kind of emotion. He'd pretty much been an open book for me to read.

Now that novel about Noah had slammed shut right in front of my face.

I didn't know the man sitting across from me, and that was painful.

"Let me just say what I have to say," I said in a pleading voice.

He shrugged, but he didn't say anything.

I decided to start at the beginning.

"When Owen and I left for Boston, I was excited to get to college. I wanted to study journalism and make my mark on the world with the written word. I had dreams of writing sensational exposés and uncovering mysteries and secrets like some of the best investigative journalists in the field right now."

"Apparently, you got disillusioned after you got to Boston," Noah said drily.

I shook my head. "I didn't. I never lost my focus. My grades were stellar, and my future looked fantastic. I never gave up on college. It gave up on me. I barely made it through my second year before I couldn't do it anymore."

"Why?" he said sharply. "If your dreams were that vivid, you certainly could have stuck out a couple more years of college."

I swallowed hard. Even though his words hurt, I guessed I understood how Noah could think that way.

I took a deep breath. "Because at the beginning of my second year, I started getting these vague symptoms. At first, I thought it was the flu, and that I was just tired after it was over. But I *stayed* tired, and by the time I'd made it through the school year, I was so exhausted, and I'd lost so much weight, that I didn't have the strength to even walk to class or around the college. My legs hurt, and I'd get these strange nosebleeds that just happened for no real reason. Owen kept nagging me to get to a doctor, and I finally did."

"What happened?" He sounded more neutral now.

"I was diagnosed with a fairly aggressive form of leukemia. They put me in the hospital and started treatment." I closed my eyes for a moment, trying not to remember how terrified and alone I'd felt back then. "One diagnosis and the bright future I'd been looking forward to was completely gone. It was physically impossible for me to start my junior year."

I didn't mention the fact that I'd been pretty certain during that particular summer that I wasn't even going to be alive when the fall semester came around.

I took a deep breath and continued. "I'm not going to lie, the treatment was brutal, and my prognosis wasn't very good."

"Cancer? Jesus! You were barely an adult," Noah said, his tone incredulous.

I smiled weakly. "Unfortunately, cancer doesn't discriminate. Owen was there for me, and I'll forever be grateful for that. I think he was the only person who kept me reasonably sane."

"Your parents—"

"Weren't there," I finished. "They didn't want to be there. They hate illness of any kind. They called once in a while from wherever they were at the time, and offered to send me a companion. I declined."

I watched his face and noticed he was no longer stoic or just angry. He looked . . . dumbfounded.

I started to rush through the last part of my explanation just to get it out while I still had the nerve. "There were times when I honestly didn't know if I was ever going to see another new day again, Noah. The chemo, medications, and radiation nearly finished me. But I guess I'm stubborn. There was a part of me that never gave up. After a year or so of treatment, I started to improve. By the end of the second year, I was in complete remission. That's why I started to travel. I didn't know when the cancer would come back, or if it would come back. So I lived in the moment, and enjoyed every single minute I had. Because that day, that moment, could very well be all I had."

He looked completely stunned, and I could tell he was searching for something to say.

"You don't have to say anything," I told him. "I just wanted you to know why I *couldn't* promise you forever. I've been in remission, but *forever* might not be in the cards for me. It isn't that I *won't* promise you that. I *can't*. It's not mine to give, but if I *was* able, there's nobody else I'd want to plan my life with but you."

Right. So that's it. Explanation complete.

I waited for him to say something, but when the silence stretched out to what seemed like an eternity, I put my mug down on the table, got up, and walked back out the front door.

CHAPTER 18

NOAH

"I need to know what's going on with Andie from your view as a physician," I told Owen with a calmness I didn't really possess at the moment.

We were seated at my kitchen table.

I'd called my brother the moment that I could manage to think straight, which, unfortunately, had come soon *after* Andie had left.

I'd hauled ass to the front door only to see the rear end of her little convertible driving away from my house.

Then I'd called Owen. I needed something, *anything* to try to make sense of what Andie had said.

"She told you?" he asked.

I nodded sharply. "It was the last thing I expected to hear."

Fuck! I'd been stunned into silence. None of what she'd said actually made sense, yet it did. I'd still been trying to digest it when she'd walked out.

"She doesn't talk about that period of her life with anybody," he shared. "The only reason I know is because I was *there*. She's been through hell, Noah. Don't blame her for not being able to see a future. At one time, she didn't have one. Medically, I wasn't sure she was going to make it. As a friend, I refused to even think about something happening to her."

Hell, I didn't blame him. I sure as hell couldn't think about it without losing my damn mind. "She was so fucking . . . young."

Owen nodded. "She was barely twenty years old when she was diagnosed. But she'd been sick even earlier than that. Leukemia symptoms can be pretty ambiguous. She thought she had some kind of virus and it was taking a long time to kick it. But she was so fatigued, and she was losing weight. I blamed myself for a long time because it took me so damn long to haul her into the hospital."

My whole body tensed. "How bad was it?" I asked him, my voice hoarse.

He lifted a brow. "The truth?"

I rubbed a hand over my face. "Yeah. I need to know."

Okay, maybe a part of me *didn't* want to know, but I squashed those reactions. If Andie could *live it*, I could deal with *hearing about it*.

"It was bad," Owen said grimly. "The first year was touch and go. She got a hell of a lot worse before she got better. She lost her hair, and I could see every bone in her body. Her doctors weren't exactly blowing smoke up her ass. Andie knew that her chances of dying were pretty high. At first, none of the treatments they tried worked. It wasn't until year two that she saw a steady improvement. But through it all, she was pretty damn brave. I'm not so sure I could have stayed as upbeat as she did."

"You never said a word about it when we talked." My voice was accusatory.

He shrugged. "She asked me not to. Andie isn't the type to ask for sympathy, and after her parents just basically wrote her off, the last thing she wanted was for anybody else to know. She said most people didn't know what to say, and it made everything awkward. I think the real truth is, she assumed she'd end up facing rejection because of her illness. I believe it was a protective instinct. Andie had all she could handle. She couldn't deal with how other people might have reacted to her illness, too."

"But right now, she's in remission?" I asked, my tone desperate.

"Andie and I went to Boston so she could get another six-month check. She was treated in an excellent cancer hospital, so she wants to keep her treatment and checkups there. She likes her doctors, and they've built trust with her over the years. This was a big hurdle for her. She just celebrated her fifth year of remission. Some doctors would say she's cured."

I eyed his serious expression. "Would *you* say she's cured?"

"I'm not an oncologist, but I would say so. Every year that passes with her being clear, the possibility of a recurrence drops. Generally, at five years, the possibility is so minuscule that she is basically cured. Don't get me wrong, it could happen, but her risk factor isn't nearly what it was during those first years."

"So why in the hell is she so reluctant to plan her future?" My body relaxed just a little.

"Think about it, Noah. She's lived five years with the fear that the cancer will come back. The treatment for two years was horrific. How long would it take you to get over that? After suffering for two years like that, and sweating recurrence for several more, would you just get to the five-year mark and blow it off? It's not going to happen. She's still scared, and understandably so."

Owen was right. And Andie had the right to still be terrified. "I wish I could have been there for her," I said, feeling guilty because I wasn't there during one of the roughest patches of her life. "What in the fuck is wrong with her parents?"

"They suck," Owen answered angrily. "They're selfish assholes, and Andie was probably better off not having them there, but I know how much their behavior hurt her. God forbid that they should have to face anything unpleasant in their lives. They never gave a shit about Andie, so I wasn't expecting them to move to Boston and hover over her, but they sure as fuck could have been there for some of it. After they abandoned her, she didn't even want to reach out to other friends, like Layla. Andie didn't want to burden anyone."

I slammed my fist against the table. "Goddammit! She could never be a burden to anyone! Why didn't she just tell me about this when we were coming back from Mexico? She let me just believe that she dropped out of college and traveled around like a gypsy because she wanted to do it. I thought she was the kind of woman who didn't have a care in the world."

"Because she *lets* everyone think that. She prefers that over people feeling sorry for her," Owen replied. "Once she recovered, she wasn't sure how much time she had left. She was a mess. So she started mindfulness meditation and tried to live her life day by day. Andie always wanted to travel the world. And since she didn't know if she was going to live another year, she got busy doing what she wanted to do before it was too late. I can't blame her for not going back to school. I know she would've liked to, but she wanted to experience . . . life."

I shook my head. "I don't blame her, either. I just wish she hadn't had to do it alone." Why waste precious time in a classroom? If I'd been in that situation, I probably would have done the same. Most people would.

However, most people absolutely wouldn't have struck out to see and experience the world all alone at the age of twenty-two.

Owen said that Andie was brave. I'd say she was pretty miraculous.

"I wanted to go with her," Owen said. "I didn't want her to be alone, especially if her time was limited. But I didn't have the money or the freedom back then to go. But I worried about her every single trip, and I made her check in with me every day."

We were quiet for a moment before I admitted, "I fucked up, Owen. I let her walk out of the house after she told me because I couldn't take everything in. Who in the fuck expects a young woman to drop a bomb on them like that? She was gone before I had a chance to say anything."

"What would you have said if you'd had the time?" he asked calmly.

I put my head down and stared at the wooden surface of the table as I clenched my fists. "I would have said that she could have told me. It wouldn't make a damn bit of difference in how I felt about her. Or maybe that's not quite the truth. I loved the way she was able to appreciate each and every day, but now that I understand why, I'm awed by her resilience, and the way she handled her life after her diagnosis. And I definitely would have told her that I didn't need forever right now. That I'd be there when and if she was ready. I just need . . . her. Maybe it sounds kind of ridiculous and poetic, and I'm not a poetry type of guy, but I think Andie and I were meant to find each other. But I fucking blew it. I let my ego replace my common sense."

"She doesn't want to hurt anyone, Noah. I think she was afraid that it would hurt more if she promised you the moon and then died on you. Yeah, she just passed a really pivotal year in her recovery, but her thinking hasn't had time to catch up with that yet."

I jerked my head up. "Don't fucking say that. She's not dying on anyone."

Christ! If I didn't know better, I'd think the crushing pain in my chest was a damn heart attack.

If she was going to get sick again, I wanted her to be with me. Period. She *needed* me by her side. Somebody other than my brother should have been there to protect her, to hold her when she was feeling weak, to be there like a permanent fixture that was never going away.

"Do you think you can hold off death?" Owen asked ruefully.

"I'd sure as hell try," I growled.

"I honestly think you would," Owen agreed. "But you're right. She's not dying on anybody. Not anytime soon, anyway. But it's going to be a while before she believes that. This was a big year for her. Year five is a huge milestone. She's still completely clean. We even picked up her five-year bracelet."

153

"Five-year bracelet?" I asked, confused.

"Every year that she's clean, Andie has gotten herself a bracelet to mark that year as cancer-free. Didn't you see them in Mexico?"

I suddenly remembered the pleasant sound of those bracelets jingling together, and understood the significance of every one of them. "I noticed. I just didn't know they meant that much to her."

"They do," Owen said solemnly. "We added the fifth one in Boston. She's reached the point where she'll just be getting a yearly check next year, and then they'll only need to see her if her symptoms return."

"They won't," I rasped. I'd make damn sure she stayed as healthy as possible.

"Noah, Andie has never really had a guy in her life except me, and I've never been anything other than a friend to her. This is all new for her. She's going to stumble a little. Can you be patient? The Sinclair men aren't actually known for taking things slow once they find the woman they're supposed to be with, but Andie is still adjusting."

It wasn't like I was all that much experienced at relationships, either, but now that I understood why Andie had still been a virgin, I wished I had been more patient. I wished that I had built up her trust instead of being ruled by my dick. "I did more than stumble," I told Owen disgustedly. "I fell flat on my ass, and I don't have the excuse that Andie does for that."

Owen chuckled. "You two really are perfect for each other."

I gave him a dirty look. "I want to be with her. It doesn't matter how long it takes for her to look at the future. I just want . . . now." I wanted every damn moment she'd spend with me.

I could keep my dick in my pants, because I was hoping to build her trust this time. If she'd trusted me completely, she would have told me the truth in the first place.

"Then tell her that," he suggested. "Andie deserves to be wined and dined, treated like she's important to a guy. She's never had that, but she should."

"I can do that." Holy hell, I *wanted* to do that.

"If you two can just be honest with each other, you'll be fine. You're going to get impatient at times, and she's still going to be afraid of a relationship. If you understand each other, you'll get through it."

"I don't plan on being impatient," I argued.

Owen shot me a doubtful look. "You will be. Look at Seth and Aiden if you need an example. Once they fell, it was hard to hold either one of them back."

"I still wish she'd told me about everything that happened to her while we were in Cancún," I said.

"Seriously, Noah? What's she supposed to say? 'Hi, I'm Andie, and I had cancer and almost died'? Who does that when they first meet someone? And consider her history. Her illness drove her *parents* away from her. Can you imagine what she'd be thinking about telling anyone else?"

"I'd like to strangle her parents," I said murderously.

"Get in line," Owen retorted. "But Andie has accepted that it's just the way her parents are made, and she's at peace with it."

There was a silent pause in the room before I said earnestly, "You've been a good friend to her, Owen."

He shook his head. "She was a good friend to me, too. It's not hard to love Andie."

"Apparently, it's pretty damn easy," I said in a self-mocking tone. "I was a goner within a day or two. She turned my whole damn world upside down."

"Do you regret that?"

I answered immediately. "No. She forced me to look at what's really important in my life, but I don't regret it."

"Just be good to her, Noah. She's one of those rare women who are worth working hard for, and I don't want to see either one of you hurt. Maybe her threat of the cancer is pretty much over, but she's still living it. She just hit year five."

"She's had enough hurt in her life," I told him reassuringly. "Like I said, you *have* been a good friend, Owen. You've taken care of her, been there for her. But I'll take it from here."

CHAPTER 19

ANDIE

Thump! Thump! Thump!

I was in a small bedroom of my cottage that I'd converted into an office and my yoga studio when I heard the pounding on my door.

Thump! Thump! Thump!

"Damn!" I cursed as I pulled myself out of my current stretching position.

I hated stopping in the middle of a yoga session, but whoever was at my door didn't sound like they were going to just go away.

Thump! Thump! Thump!

"You could use the doorbell," I mumbled to myself, annoyed as I rose to my feet.

It wasn't terribly late, but I didn't usually get visitors after dinner unless I knew they were coming.

I was hoping it was Owen or Layla, because I wasn't exactly wearing visitor attire. I was dressed in a pair of skin-tight, stretchy yoga pants and a breathable tank top.

I jogged awkwardly to the door and yanked it open. I planned on giving somebody an earful for pounding on my door instead of simply ringing the doorbell.

However, I couldn't say a word as I saw exactly who was knocking like a maniac.

Noah.

He hadn't had a thing to say when I'd visited him earlier in the day. What did he want now?

"Noah," I finally choked out breathlessly.

He looked dangerously pissed off, but I had no idea why he would be.

The man barged in like he owned my place. "We need to talk," he said in a fierce voice that surprised me. "Did you think I was just going to walk away after the bomb you dropped on me?"

Well . . . yes. I actually *had* expected him to back off, and his silence earlier had just solidified that assumption.

"Honestly, yes."

He turned to look at me. "You thought wrong. Jesus, Andie. It took me forever just to process everything you said."

"I told you that you didn't need to say anything."

He sent me a sharp glance. "Oh, I have plenty to say. I'm not going anywhere. You're stuck with me, whether you want me to be around or not."

My heart started to soar, and I had to pull it back down to earth. "It wasn't my intention to make you feel sorry for me."

"I don't feel sorry for *you*. I feel sorry for *myself*. Somehow, I managed to let the best thing that ever happened to me just walk away. I won't make the same mistake again." His voice was harsh, and his eyes were wild with some kind of emotion I couldn't decipher.

Noah was . . . different. Almost . . . bossy.

I wasn't sure if that was good or bad.

Flustered, I walked into the kitchen. "Would you like something to drink?"

"Several shots of tequila?" he grumbled.

I smiled. "You're out of luck. I'm out. But Owen left some beer."

"I'll take one," he replied.

I was still a little sweaty from my yoga, so I grabbed myself a water, and got Noah a bottle of beer.

I handed it to him. "Have a seat," I suggested, waving at the table.

"I don't know if I can sit," he said, his voice still irritable.

I sat and watched him prowl around my kitchen as I chugged some water.

I was nervous, and almost wished I had that tequila right now, too.

"Is everything okay?" I finally asked, concerned.

"No. Nothing is okay, Andie. I spoke to Owen after you came to the house. He told me what you'd been through, without candy coating it. I've been fucked ever since. Do you have any idea how much I hate what happened to you? I hate that you were alone. I hate the fact that cancer almost took your life. I hate everything right now."

I smiled because he *did* look like he was pissed off at the whole entire world, and I'd never seen him like this before. "Do you hate me, too?"

"Hell, no. I feel like an asshole over the way I treated you, but in my defense, I could have never even imagined why you feel the way you do. But I did get to know you, and I should have known that there was more to the story. Why didn't you say something?"

"I almost did," I confessed. "But when you said you couldn't imagine your life without me in it anymore, I thought telling you everything would be pretty selfish."

He finally plopped in a chair at the end of the table. "So you thought it would be better for me if you just dropped the whole relationship?"

I shrugged. "Maybe." I hadn't wanted him to hurt more if it turned out that I didn't have forever.

"Well, dammit! It's *not* better. I'm willing to wait. I'll give you time. We'll spend time together. Date like normal people do. But I'm not walking away again. Not unless you tell me that you can't stand the sight of me anymore."

Noah had this whole bossy alpha thing going on, and I had to admit that it was attractive on him. It was a hidden part of him that I'd never seen before, and I was intrigued. "Will I get any say in all of this?"

"Yes. No. I'm not sure if I want you to have any say. You might say no."

He looked so torn that I had to hold back a grin. Not that there was anything remotely funny about how he was acting, but part of me was blissfully captivated by the fact that a man like Noah felt this way about . . . me.

Why?

How?

How wonderful . . .

If only I wasn't afraid I'd die on him and leave him devastated. Just the thought of that tore me to pieces.

I'd had a lot of time to accept my possible fate, which was why I tried to live as many meaningful days as possible. It was also the reason I avoided any emotional entanglements.

My instinct was to shut Noah down and kick him out of my house.

My emotions were urging me to be as truthful with him as possible.

"I'd like to date," I admitted. "I haven't done much of that. A little bit in high school, and a few times in college during the first year, but I never really found anyone I wanted a second date with. Then, when I got sick, I was either unable or unwilling once I got my prognosis." I took a deep breath to calm my frantic heartbeat before I added, "I've never really had an opportunity to live like a normal person since the moment I got my diagnosis."

"It's time, Andie. *You* need to jump back into life, too. Owen told me that the chances of you coming out of remission are pretty slim now. And even if they weren't, I'd still want to be with you. A day with you is better than a million days with anybody else. I'm more than willing to take any chance if it means spending more time with you."

Unwanted tears filled my eyes, and I felt bombarded by so many emotions for this man that they all seemed to ball up in my throat, making it impossible to speak. Nobody in my life had ever wanted to be with me that much. "I'm scared," I said in a pitiful voice that didn't sound like my own.

Rationally, I knew I'd just passed year five of being cancer-free, but my heart was still afraid of what being involved with someone like Noah might mean. I wanted to protect him from tragedy, yet I wasn't sure it was the right thing for me to do now.

"You have a right to be scared, sweetheart," he said mildly. "I get it. I'm not going to rush you. No more thinking with my dick. No sex. I promise. Let's take it day by day. I just want to *be there* for every single one of those days. I'm not going to bullshit you and say that I don't want forever with you, but I'm good if we just take it one day at a time. All of those days will turn into forever, eventually."

My hands were shaking as I raised the water to my lips and drank, stalling for time.

What if I did try to step back into a normal life?

What if we just dated, and didn't rush anything?

What if we just took it one day at a time?

What if we didn't think about tomorrow?

I'm still going to fall in love with him.

Truth was, I'd *already* fallen. *Really, really hard.*

I just wasn't sure if I wanted him to fall in love with me. "I don't want to destroy your life if I get sick again," I said with brutal honesty.

"You're not going to ruin my life, Andie. And you're not going to get sick again. Anything can happen. I could walk out of this house right now and get hit by a bus. I could fall in the shower and crack my skull. Tomorrow is never a guarantee for any of us. I learned that when my mother died. She was young. It shouldn't have happened. But it did."

He was right. I knew he was. But that didn't mean I wasn't worried. In the past, the only person I had to worry about was myself. I'd always known I wasn't going to drag anybody down with me.

Reasonably, I *did* know that my chances of the cancer coming back were small. I'd crossed the five-year mark. I probably had the same chance of the leukemia recurring as I did of having some kind of accident and dying.

To really live life, I was going to have to take some risks, and the odds were on my side.

It wasn't like Noah was proposing marriage, or something heavy. I answered before I changed my mind. "Okay. Let's do it. What are the rules?"

He shook his head. "No rules except one."

"Tell me."

"It has to be *just* you and me, Andie. I know that's kind of a commitment, but we have to be exclusive. I can't go into town and see you with somebody else. It would kill me," he said in a low, guttural tone.

Really, I couldn't stand to see him with another woman, either. So that was a pretty easy condition. "Done. But that goes both ways." I didn't want to see him cuddling up to another female, either.

He let out a huge breath. "Thank God. I don't want another woman. I never have."

I suddenly wanted to weep with happiness. How had I gotten lucky enough to capture Noah Sinclair's attention? Granted, he was a little overwhelming at the moment, but he was the most amazing guy I'd ever known.

And he's actually going to be mine—at least, he will be for now.

"Now that we have *that* out of the way, tell me how in the hell you ever got through your adult life so far, because it seems to me that it really sucked." He slugged down more of his beer and then looked at me expectantly.

I squirmed. I wasn't all that used to talking really honestly about my life with anybody except Owen. "I didn't think about tomorrow," I explained. "Really, I was a wreck in the beginning. My anxiety was out of control, and I had nightmares about dying almost every night. I started meditation, yoga, and relaxation techniques once my health started to improve. It helped. And traveling kept my mind off the thought of dying. As long as I kept moving, and I was busy, I was okay."

"Owen said that you get a bracelet for every year that you're cancer-free."

I held my arm out to show him the five bangle bracelets on my wrist. "I just got my last one when I was in Boston. Getting these became a celebration of sorts for me. Another year clean, another bracelet. It's just symbolic, but they're a reminder of how far I've come."

I watched as he looked at the engraving on every single one of them before he said, "I wish I would have known you during those years."

"I don't. I looked like a dead woman walking. I lost my hair. I had bruises and wounds everywhere from treatment. And I was so skinny that it was one of the only times in my life when I didn't have to worry about my ass being huge."

He shot me a warning look. "I love your ass, small or big. Doesn't matter. And do you really think I would have given a damn about how you looked?"

I slowly shook my head. "No."

His words touched me somewhere deep inside my soul. He had to be one of the few men in the world who *wouldn't* give a damn what my body looked like. Noah would find a way to love it.

"You'll have to love my ass big," I informed him. "I like my food too much to give it up now."

"I don't want you to give anything up to be with me. I'd never want that." He paused before he asked, "Can you stay in one place for a while so we can do some stuff together? Either that, or take me with you."

"What about your work?"

"I decided to work slow on my next project. I need a break. I recently discovered I've come into some money. I'm considering buying my own jet so I can eventually do some traveling. I'd take you anywhere you want to go." He was joking, but there was seriousness in his voice, too.

"*Some* money?" I teased. "You're one of the wealthiest guys on the planet."

"Okay. *A lot* of money," he conceded. "I can afford to take some time off. I finished the dating app, and I'm not in any hurry to start something new."

I surveyed him curiously. He appeared to be totally unfazed at the idea of knocking off work, which was a surprise. "I wasn't planning anything in the near future. I was going to stay fairly local. I haven't been to San Diego for a while. And there's a couple of places I could hit here in Citrus Beach to blog about."

"I'm willing to give you a second opinion," he offered enthusiastically.

I snorted. "I'll get you food addicted eventually."

"So, what time do you want me to pick you up for dinner tomorrow?"

My heart sank. "I can't tomorrow. I'm having dinner with Layla."

"Saturday night?"

That was the day after tomorrow, and even though he'd phrased it like a question, I was pretty sure that Noah wasn't taking *no* for an answer. Even if he had to go through next year until he had a date.

There was something hot about his pushy new attitude. Obviously, he'd always been *quietly* determined, but he was getting *doggedly . . .* persistent.

"I can do that. There's a new steakhouse in town—"

"I'll make a reservation for seven."

CHAPTER 20

ANDIE

"What are you doing?" Noah asked as he entered the house and closed the sliding glass door behind him. "You look like your brain is a million miles away right now."

"Sorry. I was just taking a minute to be still," I explained as I smiled at him.

Noah and I had been officially dating for a couple of weeks now, and we'd been pretty busy. Not to mention the fact that we had the whole Sinclair family in the backyard today since Noah was hosting the family barbecue.

He shot me a quizzical look. "You're not still. You're moving."

I was currently slicing avocados, so he was right. But . . . "You don't have to be *physically still*. Being still is like clearing your mind. With all of the chaos, negativity, and technology in the world, it's easy to forget that sometimes it's relaxing to just focus on your breathing and open yourself up to the world around you. It's good for stress."

"*Are* you stressed?" he asked as he came around the counter.

I chuckled. "No. Not really. It's just habit so I don't get stressed."

He looked so worried that something might be wrong that it melted my heart.

The last few weeks had been anything but full of stressful activity.

We'd eaten a lot, in various places. Every day, we found time to take a walk on the beach, swim, go for a ride on the boat he'd recently purchased, fish, talk, or just find something new to learn.

Every day was an adventure when I was with Noah, no matter what we were doing.

And I fell more in love with the sometimes aggravating, sweet, tender, handsome man every single day.

"What else can I help with?" he asked as he wrapped his powerful arms around me from behind.

"Nothing. I've got everything under control. How's the fish doing?"

He'd put the whitefish on the grill. I'd suggested making a massive batch of fish tacos for dinner, an alternative to the usual hamburgers, hot dogs, or steaks.

His entire family had been pretty enthusiastic about the idea.

"It should be done shortly," he told me as he nuzzled the side of my neck.

I inhaled a sharp gasp, my body responding to his warm breath hitting the sensitive skin.

"Stop that," I scolded weakly, wishing his entire family *wasn't* sitting outside on the patio. "Your family is here."

However, that wasn't the real reason he had to stop. My poor body had been in a heightened state of sexual frustration for the last couple weeks. There was only so much I could take.

Noah had done exactly as he promised. He hadn't thought with his dick once since we'd started to date. We touched a lot. He was affectionate, but he hadn't tried to get me back into his bed.

He cut things off if they got too heavy.

And it was driving me crazy.

I knew he was taking it slow, trying not to rush me, but I was more than ready to take as many steps as necessary to get him naked again.

I realized I'd be taking one step further into commitment, but I was starting to accept the fact that no matter what happened in the future, Noah and I were going to go through it together. We both cared too damn much to walk away.

Dammit! I was ready to take that leap of faith.

I just wasn't sure if Noah was, too.

Unfortunately, *now* wasn't the time for *that*. Not with his entire family here.

When he let go of me, he moved off to the side, put his elbows on the counter, and watched me.

It used to make me uncomfortable when he did that, but now I was used to it, and I kind of liked the way he looked at me like I was the most important thing in the room to him. He certainly wasn't the type of guy who would ever have a wandering eye.

"Are you sure there's nothing I can do?"

"Positive," I assured him. "Everything is pretty much done. We just need to carry it all outside. I hope your family likes everything."

Okay, I *was* just a little bit nervous because we had his family all together at his place. I'd met them all as an adult at one time or the other over the last few weeks, but it was a little intimidating to have them all in *one place at one time.*

Everyone had been more than welcoming to me, but I wasn't used to large family gatherings. And I couldn't help but wonder what they thought of their older brother's new girlfriend.

I guessed I really wanted them to like me. Family was important to Noah, and the last thing I wanted was disapproval from them.

"Hey," he said in a soft baritone. "Are you nervous?"

"Yes . . . No . . . I don't know," I said in a rush. "What if they don't think we belong together or something?"

I wanted them to be here, but maybe I was a little bit anxious. Most of them knew my history now. Maybe they didn't want their brother to be with a woman who might eventually drag him down with her illness.

He put a hand on my wrist to still my slightly frantic motions. I hadn't even noticed that the avocado pieces were getting pretty small until he stopped my actions. "Andie, my family isn't like that. All of them are grateful that you're willing to take me on. Nobody is going to judge you."

"They are going to want whatever is best for you, Noah," I told him.

"That would be you," he said simply. "You make me happy, and they know that. And if a single one of them disagrees, which they won't, I don't give a damn. Do you think they don't know that all of the positive changes I've made in my life are because of you?"

"I'm sorry," I said as I threaded my fingers through his. "I guess I just don't know how to do this whole 'meet the family' thing. It's all so different for me. I'm used to being alone."

"And my family is overwhelming," he added.

"They're wonderful," I corrected. "It's just a little daunting for a woman who really has no family of her own."

Honestly, I loved watching Noah interact with his family. They joked and teased each other, but the love within the entire Sinclair family was pretty obvious.

"We accept new people without a whole lot of judgment," he said lightly.

I nodded. "I know. It's not them. It's me. I'm excited that they're here, and I'll get over the nerves."

"They won't let you be a stranger for long," he said, sounding amused as he fingered my chakra bracelet. "You have a meaning for the other bracelets. Is there a meaning to this one?"

I shrugged as I released his hand and went back to my chopping in a less aggressive manner. I didn't really want guacamole by the time I was done slicing. "Not really. It's a chakra bracelet. One of my first trips was to India. I went to an ashram for a while to help me hone my meditation skills. It was good for me. I felt a lot more balanced and hopeful after my visit than I was before I got there."

He lifted a brow. "What's an ashram and a chakra?"

I laughed. "An ashram is kind of like a hermitage. A place to go back to the basics and find spiritual guidance."

"Hindu?"

"The one I visited welcomes people from all walks of life and all philosophies. I guess I just went there to try to find myself again after those tough years of treatment."

"And did you find yourself?" he asked huskily.

"Not exactly. But it helped. I spent a lot of time practicing meditation and self-reflection. I stopped feeling sorry for myself and learned to be grateful for what I had."

"Where does the bracelet fit in?"

"The simplest way to explain it is that the bracelet has healing stones. I mostly bought this one because it reminded me to keep going back to the basics when everything got too overwhelming, and because it was pretty. I'm not much into the belief in the stones themselves, but I do like nice, colorful things."

He chuckled as he looked me up and down. "I noticed."

I smirked. "Are you mocking my dress?"

I'd put on a bright-yellow sundress earlier, and I loved it.

"Not at all," he said immediately. "You look like a bright ray of sunshine, sweetheart."

I sighed. Would there ever be a day that Noah couldn't make me feel beautiful? Fortunately, I highly doubted it.

I put the last sliced avocado into a large bowl with the rest of them. "I think we're ready."

"I'll take that," he insisted as he grabbed the bowl. "Go outside and let Aiden pour you a glass of wine. He's playing bartender. You've done enough today. I'll grab Seth, Eli, and Owen to help me bring everything out."

I tried to protest, but he nudged me toward the sliding glass door, so I stepped out into the mild Southern California afternoon.

"Andie! Come sit down and have a drink," Riley called as I moved toward the crowd.

I smiled at her as she patted the empty lounger next to her.

Noah's backyard was enormous and beautifully landscaped. The large pool was the focal point, but there were numerous places to gather around it. Beyond that, there was nothing but ocean.

"Thanks," I said to Riley as I plopped my ass down on the lounger, and Aiden handed me a glass of red wine.

"Noah said you liked red," he said in a jovial tone.

"I do. Thank you."

I certainly couldn't complain about the Sinclair service. I had to wonder if Aiden had already poured the wine before I'd stepped outside.

I took a sip as I watched Aiden walk back to the barbecue grill to check on the fish.

"It's a little mind boggling, right?" Riley commented, her tone brimming with laughter. "I know the first few Sinclair family barbecues were a little intimidating to me. I wasn't used to this much family in one area."

I looked around at all of the activity. Aiden was minding the fish on the grill while he had an animated conversation with Owen, Seth, and Eli Stone. Aiden's wife, Skye, was in the pool with their daughter, Maya. Jade was keeping them company at the side of the pool.

Everyone looked so happy just to be . . . together.

"You don't have family?" I asked her curiously.

"None that I actually want to claim," she said drily. "Except for my brothers. And they're out of the country a lot."

"My parents are always gone," I told her. "And I'm an only child."

"So this is probably really weird for you," she said empathetically. "Don't worry. You'll get used to it. I actually look forward to all the family gatherings now. The Sinclairs have a way of drawing you in until you feel like part of the family."

Riley was so nice that it was hard to be nervous around her. "Thanks. I already like everyone. I knew most of them when I was younger, but it's been a long time."

"We already adore you," she informed me. "After what you've done for Noah, we're all grateful."

"I just went on a vacation with him."

"He's changed, Andie. I mean he's *really* changed. He's spending time with his siblings, and they're thrilled to have him back as a brother. I'm not sure I really saw him smile until he came back from Cancún. Now he can't seem to stop smiling. You make him happy. You've pulled him out of his office and helped him rejoin the real world. Don't act like your influence didn't make a difference. The man has learned how to play. That's monumental for Noah."

"Was it really that bad?" I asked.

"Horrible," she answered. "Everybody was worried about him, and with good reason."

I pretty much knew it wasn't good from what Owen had told me. "He was always a workaholic, but he had to be when his siblings were young. I hadn't seen him for years before we ended up in Cancún together. He didn't look well."

"You wouldn't know he looked like hell just over a month ago by looking at him today. He's crazy about you."

I sighed. "I'm crazy about him, too."

"I'm not going to tiptoe around like I don't know what you've been through. All of us know, and we hate what happened to you," Riley said bluntly. "I just want you to know that if you ever want to talk about it, I'm here for you. We all are."

I was so touched that I could feel the tears welling up in my eyes. "Thanks."

Riley was offering me friendship, family, and acceptance without a single reservation.

I wasn't quite sure how to handle that, but it felt so damn good that I wasn't about to shy away from it.

"I'm ready for those tacos." Riley sat up as she spoke and smiled at me.

I grinned back at her. If she was that enthusiastic about food, we were going to be friends.

CHAPTER 21

ANDIE

"Where in the world are we going?" I asked Noah curiously as I rode beside him in his SUV.

It had been a few weeks since we'd hosted the barbecue at Noah's, and I was no longer nervous about his family.

I saw all of them often, and I was always greeted like family. Riley, Jade, and Skye had become my friends, and we got together as often as possible to shop, eat, or just hang out and talk.

The days had flown by, and it was a beautiful spring day in Southern California. Noah had been driving for a while, and I knew we were somewhere near San Diego, but other than that, I had no idea where he was taking me.

He'd been closemouthed about our destination. All he'd requested was for me to dress casually.

I'd donned some jeans and a short-sleeved, multicolored spring top. At his insistence, I'd put on a sturdy pair of shoes.

"We're almost there. Don't be so impatient," he teased.

Jokingly, I let out a huff and relaxed back against the leather passenger seat.

Noah and I had gotten into a routine.

We worked in the morning and generally met up in the early afternoon. Our days usually ended with both of us being sexually frustrated when we parted in the evening, but other than that, I couldn't complain about a single moment I spent with him.

I was pretty sure we both wanted to take our relationship further, but Noah hadn't budged an inch off his original promise.

Dammit!

Why isn't he making a move?

The intense chemistry we had was always there, always present, but he still hadn't gone beyond tender kisses and affectionate gestures.

I was almost out of patience.

I wanted to be with Noah so badly that every moment I spent with him was starting to become torturous.

Not that I wasn't willing to endure a little torment just to be with him, but it was starting to get ridiculous.

My body was clamoring for his, and I needed him. Desperately. I wanted to crawl inside Noah and never leave.

He's holding back for me.

I knew it.

I sensed it.

I just wasn't sure how else to prove to him that I wasn't going to shy away from the intimacy.

There wasn't a single doubt in my mind that I wanted to be with him for every tomorrow that I had.

I fingered the five bracelets on my wrist absently.

It has been over five years.

Slowly, I was getting over my fear and starting to live in reality.

How could I not? Noah Sinclair was a pretty amazing, real-world existence to spend my time in.

I felt alive, animated, and eager to see what each new day was going to bring our way.

I was in love with him in a way I'd never experienced.

Soul deep.

All-consuming.

Heart, soul, body, and mind.

That love was starting to eclipse most of the fears that I'd had in the beginning. Maybe we didn't talk about it, but I was getting to the point that I couldn't see any kind of future . . . without him.

He was changing, too.

The man had become very comfortable in his own skin now. He knew when to stop working, and he didn't seem to be having any difficulty putting his computer aside after he'd worked hard all morning.

He spent more time with his family, acting like a big brother instead of a father. I could tell that he'd stopped putting any kind of distance between his family and himself.

Eli had been helping Noah, showing him how to handle his fortune, and Noah, brilliant man that he was, was becoming a very savvy investor with guidance from Eli Stone and his half brother, Evan.

There was very little hesitance in Noah anymore.

He knew what he wanted.

Luckily, the thing he seemed to want the most was . . . *me.*

I just wished he'd get to the point where he had to have carnal knowledge of me, too.

The more confident he'd become, the bossier he seemed to be. But I could handle *that* a whole lot better than I could deal with the lost look he'd had when he'd first been jolted into the real world.

He and Owen talked a lot, maybe because they could relate to each other about catching up with the rest of the world.

My wayward thoughts jumped back into the moment when Noah turned into what appeared to be some kind of ranch or farm.

"Okay, you're killing me here," I whined. "What *are* we doing?"

There had never been this much mystery about how we were going to spend our afternoon.

Usually we picked a simple event where we could just spend time together, or we ate somewhere that I could incorporate into my blog.

He parked his vehicle at the end of the driveway in what looked like a makeshift dirt parking lot.

Noah turned to look at me once he'd shut the engine off. "You'll see. It wouldn't be a surprise if I tell you everything."

I snorted. "But you're going to eventually tell me, right?"

He didn't answer as he got out of the SUV and jogged around to open the passenger door. "Get out," he instructed, taking the sting out of the command as he reached for my hand.

Once we'd walked past a big barn, I could see the . . .

"Horses," I said breathily as I gazed at the pasture full of the grazing animals.

"I think you once told me that riding a horse on the beach was one of the things you really wanted to experience," he said gently.

"I do." I couldn't keep the longing out of my voice. "But you said you weren't the cowboy type."

He shrugged his massive shoulders and grinned at me. "Turns out, you don't really have to be a cowboy to ride. They take beginners. We'll have a guide, but we're going private. I bought out all the other tour spots. This excursion goes along a riverbed and comes out on the beach."

My heart started to race as I looked up at him. "Really?"

I'd never imagined that there was actually a place where we could ride on a beach in this area.

Guess I was wrong.

What kind of research had Noah needed to do to find out how he could make one of my dreams happen for real?

"Really," he said with a nod.

"And you're okay with doing this?" It wouldn't mean much if he wasn't into it, too. I'd never want Noah to do anything that he wasn't excited about doing himself.

He'd spent enough time catering to others.

"Baby, I'm ecstatic because I'm going to be watching you realize one of the experiences you want to have." He didn't look the least bit reluctant.

I love you. I love you so much!

The words wanted to escape from my lips so badly. The need to say them was pressing on my heart. "Thank you," I murmured, playing it safe. I wasn't sure if Noah was ready for me to blurt out those emotions.

Just his actions showed me how much he cared about me every day. But he hadn't said the words, either.

I was completely mortified when I started to cry. It wasn't a delicate, tears-are-falling-from-my-eyes-silently type of emotion.

Instead, it was a sobbing-like-my-entire-world-is-falling-apart kind of deal.

"Andie, what's wrong?" Noah's tone was worried and demanding as he wrapped his arms around me.

"I can't believe you arranged all this for me." I sobbed harder as I buried my face against his chest.

So many emotions were pouring from my soul that I couldn't have stopped myself if I tried.

I cried for every bit of pain I'd suffered during my treatment.

I cried for every year I'd spent trying not to worry.

I cried for everything Noah had lost during his childhood and adult years.

I cried for any hurt I'd ever caused this amazing man because I'd been so reluctant to really love *anyone*.

I cried for the loneliness I'd felt on my travels, and when I'd felt lost.

But mostly, I cried because I felt so damn lucky to have what I now shared with Noah.

Connection.

Intimacy.

The man generally cared more about my happiness than his own, and that shook me to my core.

I'd pretty much spent my entire life alone, and I'd had no idea what it would be like to be so close to someone.

To put it simply, it was totally . . . sublime.

"Hey, don't cry, Andie. This whole thing wasn't meant to upset you," he crooned in a low, soothing tone.

"I'm happy," I choked out as I tried to recover my sanity.

"It sure as hell doesn't seem like it," he said despondently as he rubbed my back.

I pulled away and wiped my tears. "I'm sorry. Everything just hit me all at once."

He frowned. "I've never seen you cry like that. I don't like it."

I beamed at him. "I'm done."

"Thank fuck!" he answered in a relieved tone.

I wrapped my arms around his neck. "I never thought I'd find somebody like you," I tried to explain.

"A crabby workaholic?" he joked as he rested his forehead against mine.

"The most incredible man in the world," I corrected. "Thank you for this, and everything else you do to make me feel special."

"You *are* special." His voice was firm and slightly censuring.

I love you.

The words were right there, hovering on my lips, but I didn't say them. Instead, I pulled his head down and kissed him, pouring everything I felt into that one embrace, and then I pulled myself out of his arms. "I guess we better get going."

"You okay?" he asked in a hoarse tone.

I took his hand as we walked to where the guide already had our horses saddled. "I'm fine, Noah. I really am."

I cooed and petted my adorable palomino before I mounted, and then I watched as Noah got onto a big black gelding.

Truthfully, I didn't have all that much experience on a horse, but riding on a beach had always looked so romantic.

Neither one of us was exactly a graceful rider, but we learned quickly, and laughed together every time we did something wrong.

When we got to the beach, Noah reached out and held my hand as we watched the motion of the waves together.

I'd never told him that part of my dream was actually riding a horse on the beach with a man I loved.

I looked at him and grinned as we moved along the sand.

Some realities were better than a dream.

CHAPTER 22

Noah

"I think I'm about to lose my damn mind, or what little of it that I have left," I confessed to Aiden and Seth as we sat around a table in Skye's restaurant.

We'd decided to meet here since all of us were hungry, and the bistro had some of the best food in town.

Andie had needed to do some work on her blog, so we'd pushed our meeting time to later in the day.

Probably better for my sanity.

"You guys look happy," Aiden said right before he wrapped his mouth around the sandwich special.

I smirked. All of Skye's specialties were piled so high that it was almost difficult to take those first few bites. "That's the problem," I grumbled. "I'm happier than I could have ever imagined. My life would be perfect if I could just lure Andie back to my bed."

Seth started to choke on his sandwich, and reached for his water. It took a few minutes before he commented. "No offense, Noah, but you can't just say that shit without some kind of warning. I'm not exactly used to you talking about getting laid."

I glared at him. "*You* talk about it." Yeah, he didn't exactly give us the details, but Seth and Aiden had no problem talking about sex in general.

"We actually *get laid*," Seth pointed out. "You generally . . . don't. And you sure as hell have never discussed it if you have."

"Well, feel free to proceed," Aiden joked. "I want to hear about it. Seth and I can share our vast knowledge about women."

I let out a bark of laughter as I dug into an enormous homemade potpie. "Your women have both of you tied around their little fingers, and you know it."

"Riley does," Seth admitted happily. "But she never uses the way I love her against me. That connection goes both ways. So what's up with you and Andie?"

"I'm having difficulties with my patience," I said uncomfortably. "I promised her that we'd take one day at a time, get to know each other, date, and that I'd stop thinking with my dick."

Aiden shot me a dubious look as he took a break from devouring his own plate of food. "You haven't had sex with her since Cancún?"

I shook my head. "No. And I'm not sure it's a good idea right now. Once we start that kind of relationship again, I'll lose my shit over her. I'll get possessive, protective, and greedy. The same way I did last time. I'll want a damn *commitment* from her." Not that I didn't already want that, but it would probably get worse if we slept together.

Both of my brothers nodded like they knew exactly what I was talking about.

Seth took another gulp of water to wash down his food before he spoke. "Look, I've seen you two together. She looks at you the same way you look at her. Maybe this isn't easy for her, either."

I didn't have a single doubt that Andie felt the same way I did, but I was worried about my timing. "You know her history, and her problem with long-term commitment."

Aiden nodded. "We get it. I can't even imagine what she's gone through. I'd probably feel the same damn way if it were me. I wouldn't want Skye to be burdened with a sick guy who might very well leave her alone in the near future. But she's passed all of the possible crisis points. The likelihood of her getting sick again is about what a normal person's odds are of getting sick. I think she'll realize that eventually, as time goes on. Right now, I think I'd just be coming to terms with the fact that I didn't have to fear that anymore. She's not a selfish person, Noah. I think the fear is all for you and not for herself."

"I already know that," I said flatly. "That's why I don't want to put any stress on her with my demands."

I knew once I possessed her body and soul, there was no going back for me. *Dammit!* There already was no going back, and I knew it. I just wasn't sure how Andie would handle it if I told her that.

"I think she can take it," Aiden said firmly. "The woman has a great head on her shoulders. And I know she's crazy about you. She's not going to walk away from you again, Noah."

Aiden touched on a nerve that I hadn't wanted to acknowledge, a thought that I'd been thinking for a while now, whether it was rational or not.

If I don't push to have sex, she won't go anywhere.

"Is that what you're worried about?" Seth asked in a serious tone.

I nodded. "Yeah. I think it is."

"Then stop being so paranoid," he directed. "That woman isn't going anywhere. She's in love with you, Noah. Head over heels. And I wouldn't be saying that if I didn't know she feels the same way you do. God knows the last thing I want is to see you end up hurt."

I raised a brow. "What makes you think that? She's never said it."

Aiden rolled his eyes with apparent annoyance. "For one, she puts up with the whole lot of us. She even seems happy to see us. Andie wants to please you, Noah. She wants to make you happy. Don't *you* see that?"

I was quiet as I looked back at the last several weeks that Andie and I had spent together.

Her desire to see me fit back into my family, in the right role for the present time, had always been one of her priorities. Not only did she put up with all of my family, but she seemed to throw herself into the group with gusto.

But there were little things, too.

She always thought about me, even when we weren't together.

If I was working, she'd bring me a coffee from the Coffee Shack that she'd picked up before coming to the house. Or she'd bring me food if she thought I hadn't eaten.

I'd mentioned the possibility of certifying to scuba dive. The next day, she was all over finding me the place and equipment to do it.

My new jet hadn't arrived yet, but Andie had been there every step of the way to push me to pick one out.

When being as rich as I was now got overwhelming, she was there to put the whole thing into perspective.

If I wanted to do *anything*, the woman was my biggest cheerleader.

She didn't ask for a single thing in return. If I did something for her, it was because I'd thought about her, too, and not because she'd asked.

Andie appreciated even the small things, like the horseback ride on the beach. Although I could have probably done *without* the crying part of the whole thing. She'd been sobbing like her heart was broken, and that had broken mine, even if it was supposedly a happy ugly-cry session.

It pissed me off that Andie had never had the attention or protection she should have had as a child, and as an adult with a life-threatening illness.

Someone should have been there for her, somebody who cared about *her* needs.

But I supposed that was a moot point, because now that I was in her life, she'd damn well get *everything* she needed. The woman would never be without a shoulder to cry on and all the emotional support she needed.

"Yeah, I see it," I finally answered. "However, I also know that she just barely passed that five-year point, and I need to give her time to adjust to having a normal life. Andie's still young. She hasn't really had any sense of normalcy as an adult."

"And you have?" Aiden said drily. "You're not that much older, and you've never really seen normal, either."

I shrugged. "Eight years. It seems like a lot."

"Do you want to get laid, or do you want to sit and wonder what her reaction will be?" Seth questioned wryly.

"I just . . . want to make her happy."

"You *both* need to be happy," Aiden said. "Now that I've gotten to know her a little, I doubt she'd be content if you weren't happy, too."

"Done. I'm fucking ecstatic. I just want it all. I can't do a damn thing about her past, but I want her present and her future to be with me."

"It will be," Seth said calmly. "Now let's get back to talking about your nonexistent sex life."

I shot him a warning glance. I wasn't in a joking mood. "I think it's too soon, but I'm not sure how much longer I can handle this."

"Believe me, we get it," Aiden said ruefully. "We've been in your position. I went through hell with Skye before we were both happy. When you find the right woman, it's hard not to want to jump all in."

"I'm already all in," I rumbled.

"Can you push a little and see how she receives it?" Seth asked. "I think you'll know."

"What if she regrets it and backtracks?"

Seth shrugged. "Then you go after her."

I finished off my potpie before I replied. "I'll always go after her. No matter how far she runs."

Aiden chuckled. "We're kind of persistent that way."

I looked from Seth to Aiden. "How in the hell did you two do it? I was there for you if you needed me, but I had no idea how you *felt* at the time. My whole damn life revolves around Andie now. My happiness depends on her and what she decides. It's hell. Did you feel that way?"

"Yep."

"Yes."

My brothers spoke those single-word answers at the same time.

Aiden took a deep breath and let it out. "I'd do it all again, over and over, if it meant I'd have Skye in the end. It will pass, Noah. I know it's not easy, but give it time. Even if you think you're at the end of your patience, you're not. You'll keep stretching it because you love her."

Aiden was right. I wasn't going to lose my shit with Andie, because she deserved better than that.

"I'll keep it together," I admitted. "Whether I'll be sane in the end is debatable."

"You look good for a guy who isn't getting any," Seth observed. "You've gained a little weight."

"Because Andie is constantly feeding me," I answered. "I started increasing my cardio every morning so I don't keep expanding. I don't need to gain any more. But I've discovered that I love to eat."

"You're a true Sinclair male now," Seth joked. "I think we all love to eat. Welcome to the wonderful world of good food."

Aiden stood since we were all done eating. "We ready to go?"

I got to my feet. "Yeah, I'm good."

"I'll give you a lift back to your office, Seth," Aiden offered.

Seth had walked to the bistro since his office was so close. But he'd need to go pick up his vehicle there before he headed home.

Aiden had picked me up so we could ride to town together.

"You know we're around if you ever need to talk. I don't know how much help I'll be, but I'm here to listen," Aiden said in a low voice as we hit the outdoors.

My relationship had changed so damn much with Seth and Aiden, and I was grateful for the offer. "Thanks."

Maybe they couldn't give me precise and easy advice, but I was glad they were there to listen when I needed to vent.

I was pretty sure I was going to need that.

CHAPTER 23

ANDIE

I'd never been a runner when it came to exercise.

Okay, I wasn't even a *jogger*.

In all honesty, I was pretty much a *walker*, and speed was negotiable, depending on how energetic I felt that particular day.

But here I was, out on the beach, bent over, holding my side, and gasping for air like I'd just run a marathon.

Ha! I hadn't even made it half a mile before I ended up so winded that I couldn't breathe.

What in the hell am I doing?

I'd become tense after completing my work, and instead of meditating or yoga, I'd thought that a nice run on the beach would help with my sexual frustration.

It . . . hadn't.

I was fairly fit, but I wasn't prepped for a damn full-out sprint.

I stood up straight, my hand still on my aching side, and started to walk it out.

A shower was definitely in order for me at the moment, and I still didn't know when Noah was going to show up.

He'd gone out with his brothers for lunch during the afternoon, but it was past dinnertime, so I was surprised that I hadn't seen him yet.

I pulled my phone out of the back pocket of my yoga pants.

Nothing. Not even a text.

I put my phone away and kept walking back toward my house.

It had been my anticipation of seeing Noah that had left me panting for breath, literally, in the first place.

One more evening of acting like a teenager on a date with a cute guy was going to kill me.

I was ready to seduce him. My only reservation was that he might think it was too soon, which could screw up what we already had.

I hadn't wanted to risk it, but I was getting desperate to spend some *adult* time with him.

In bed.

Under the covers.

On top of the covers.

On a kitchen counter.

The couch, maybe?

I thought I was throwing him enough signals; he should be seeing the big green light by now.

My respirations were returning to normal, and I dropped my hand from my side.

I'll live. I just need to be patient. I'd do decades in hell if it means I eventually get Noah.

I wondered if I actually needed to tell him I was ready.

For anything? Am I ready to give him forever?

Over the last several weeks, Noah and I had both subtly changed.

He was becoming more comfortable with himself and figuring out what his priorities were in his life. He worked, but he did a lot of playing, too, and he'd figured out that he desperately needed to slow

189

it down. At least for a while. I'd figured out that the whole bossiness thing was an inherent part of his personality. It had just been fairly absent while we were in Cancún because he'd been pretty lost. Noah was a leader. He'd had to be. However, I'd never had to get in his face for being high-handed, because he was also fundamentally kind and thoughtful.

Actually, he could take that whole alpha, demanding thing into the bedroom, and I certainly wouldn't argue with him.

Don't. Go. There.

I stopped myself just before I started having yet another sexual fantasy, forcing myself to focus on getting back to my house. Sunset was starting, and although there wasn't a ton of crime in Citrus Beach, I'd rather not be alone on the beach after dark.

As soon as my little cottage was in sight, I noticed what appeared to be a male figure on my back patio.

Noah?

My heart rate increased just at the thought of seeing him again, and it had been less than twenty-four hours since we'd parted.

Whether we had sex or not, I wanted to be with him.

See how his day had gone.

Listen to that sexy baritone say my name.

Cuddle up to the warmth of his body.

See him smile.

I squinted into the fading light.

Not . . . Noah.

When I got to the gate, I swung it open and stepped into my backyard.

"Owen?" I said, surprised.

My best friend had found himself a house, and had been able to move in as a renter while the sale was closing. He'd been in his new place since right after we'd returned from Boston.

Since Noah and I were together, he didn't stop by without calling . . . usually.

He looked relieved to see me. "I'm glad you're home. I've been ringing the doorbell in the front, and you weren't answering, so I decided to check the back. I was afraid you weren't here."

I'd known Owen since we were in grade school, so it wasn't difficult for me to discern that something wasn't right with him. "What's wrong?"

"Aiden and Noah had an accident. They're at the hospital. I thought you'd want to go with me."

I froze as I reached him. *What the hell?* "Oh, my God, Owen. Are they okay?"

He shook his head. "I don't know. The police called Skye, and she's on her way there. The only thing the police would tell her was that Noah was in the ICU, and Aiden is in the ER right now."

My entire body started to shake. "He would have called if he was able. I know he would have," I said tremulously. "I'm coming. Let me grab my purse and lock the door."

Every action was automatic.

I certainly couldn't think rationally.

I had to assume that Noah was bad enough that he couldn't use his phone.

Owen followed me through the back door, and I locked it behind him and grabbed my purse. We exited in the front where Owen's car was parked.

The hospital was on the other side of downtown, but it wouldn't take us long to get there.

"Buckle up," Owen insisted as he pulled out of the driveway.

I reached for my seat belt in a daze. "They have to be all right," I said with a calmness I definitely didn't feel.

Owen had two brothers who were injured. I was *not* going to lose it in front of him.

I couldn't.

I had to keep it together for Owen's sake.

"At least I know they weren't on the freeway. The cops gave Skye the location of the accident," Owen said pensively. "Not that people don't haul ass on that main road away from town, but I know that Aiden wouldn't be doing that. There's too many kids around at that time of day."

"It must have happened a few hours ago," I said absently. "He was supposed to meet me at my place when he was done meeting up with Seth and Aiden. What about Seth?"

"It was just Aiden and Noah, as far as I know."

Seth must have driven separately, or been dropped somewhere in town before Aiden and Noah headed toward home. Noah had told me he was riding with Aiden when I'd spoken to him earlier on the phone.

"Does Seth know?" I asked nervously.

Owen nodded. "Skye was going to call Seth and Jade on the way to the hospital. She wanted to see what was going on before she called Brooke."

It was the rational thing to do, since Jade's twin sister was living on the other side of the country with her husband.

"We can't panic until we know the whole situation," Owen said, sounding like he was trying to convince himself to stay calm. "Mostly likely, they're both fine."

ICU. ICU. ICU.

Intensive care.

I'd spent enough time in the critical-care unit to know that whatever had happened, it wasn't good, but I wasn't going to voice my fears to Owen.

I turned my face toward the passenger window as tears spilled from my eyes.

The wait to get to the hospital was agonizing when we had no idea how either of the guys were doing.

I wished that I would have told Noah how much I loved him. I should have. But I didn't.

I'd been waiting for *him* to say it, but he hadn't.

What if he's not okay? What in the hell am I going to do?

He should have heard those words a long time ago. I'd certainly felt them.

Why didn't I tell him? I'm ready for anything he wants. I'm ready for a . . . future.

Funny that I could suddenly have *that* epiphany when I wasn't sure if *he* had forever.

Dammit!

Covertly, I swiped the tears from my cheeks.

It had never occurred to me that someday, it could be *Noah* who was lying in a hospital bed with his life hanging in the balance.

He was too full of life, too bold, too full of energy and light.

Tomorrow is never a guarantee.

Noah had said that, and he was right. All this time, I'd only imagined *myself* getting ill. Not *him*.

I was the one I'd always imagined who might leave *him*.

I wrapped my arms around my body.

Please don't leave me, Noah. Please.

I couldn't even imagine a life without him anymore. He'd turned my life upside down, taught me how to love, showed me what real love should be like.

He'd love me even if I did get sick.

Noah was just stubborn that way when he cared about someone. He'd stick to me like superglue, no matter the circumstances.

I breathed a sigh of relief when we pulled in to the hospital.

I'd been an idiot not to just jump into a relationship with Noah headfirst, simply because of my fear.

If I'd just ridden the feelings I had for him, let them just come naturally, and allowed myself to act on every single one of them, I wouldn't be worried about the fact that Noah might not know that I loved him.

I just need one more chance. Please give me one more chance.

Owen and I didn't say a word once he'd found a parking spot. He just put his arm around me, and we sprinted for the emergency room.

CHAPTER 24

ANDIE

"Everybody needs to just go home. Get out, and go get some sleep. Stop fussing over me. I'm going to live until tomorrow."

I let out the huge breath I'd been holding as I heard Noah's comment all the way from outside his room.

If he was that grumpy, he was going to be okay, right?

Aiden was down in the ER getting a laceration sewn up before he could go home. All of his tests had been negative, so he'd be discharged. Skye and Owen were sitting with him.

Seth, Riley, Jade, and Eli were inside Noah's room in the ICU right now, but would probably be leaving soon since Noah had just given them their walking orders.

I sagged against the wall, relief flooding over me.

Aiden had told me that Noah was okay, and that they were keeping him overnight in the ICU so he could be watched carefully through the night. He'd been banged up pretty bad, and he'd lost consciousness for a brief period of time after the accident. There was nothing showing up on his tests, but they were observing Noah because he had a concussion.

I hadn't been completely convinced that Noah would be okay.

Which was why I'd rushed up to the third floor in the elevator and hauled ass to Noah's room once I'd been allowed in.

His cranky words to his relatives, as weird as it might sound, were music to my ears.

Oh, my God. He really is going to be fine.

I couldn't wait a second longer, so I stumbled into his room, saw his gorgeous face, and tried to hold back a sob of relief.

I failed miserably at keeping my emotions in check.

"Noah?" I choked out.

I froze as I got to the end of his bed.

His hazel eyes locked with mine. "Andie? What's wrong, baby?"

"I love you." The words fell from my lips without my really think-ing about the appropriateness of saying them with most of his family watching.

"Everybody out . . . now!" he growled, his eyes never leaving mine.

Every visitor except me scrambled for the door and left without another word spoken.

I continued, "I was so scared."

He opened his arms. "Come here." It was a command, and his tone was persuasive.

I moved toward him. "You're hurt." I wanted to throw myself in his arms, but I could tell he was bruised and battered.

There was a sutured laceration near his forehead, bruising all over his face, and God only knew where else he was messed up.

He grimaced as he leaned forward, grabbed my hand, and pulled with so much force that I had no choice but to lean down and let him draw me into his embrace.

Tears poured from my eyes, and I didn't know what else to say. I felt so much that I just couldn't put everything into words.

Noah wrapped his arms around me as he crooned, "Don't cry, sweetheart. I'll be out of here tomorrow."

I let him hold me for a glorious moment, and I allowed myself to feel the comfort of that embrace before I pulled back to look at his face. "You're hurt," I said tearfully as I stroked a gentle hand through his hair.

"It's nothing," he said smoothly. "Now would you like to tell me again what you said when you first came in?"

"I love you," I repeated without hesitation. "I should have told you that a long time ago. You should have known. I was terrified that I wouldn't have a chance to say it."

"I'm so sorry, baby," he said huskily. "Aiden and I didn't think about grabbing our phones from the car when the ambulances got there. If I'd known you were worried, I would have found a damn phone somewhere. The accident just happened so fast."

I knew that the rest of the family had only beat Owen and me to the hospital by a matter of minutes. So none of them had gotten the chance to call, either. "It wasn't your fault," I told him as I pulled away from him and moved the chair up beside the bed so my face would be close to his as I sat. "What happened?"

He took my hand and threaded his fingers through mine. "Some idiot ran a red light and smashed into our passenger side. He was going way too fast. *He* was okay, but Aiden and I got pummeled."

The passenger side? *His side* of the vehicle. "Are you sure you're okay?"

"I look worse than I feel."

I shot him a dubious glance. "Liar. I can see that you're hurting."

He let out a masculine sigh. "Okay. My right side is killing me because it took the brunt of the impact, and my ribs are all bruised up. But that's the worst of it. I promise." Noah hesitated a moment before he asked, "Is it all right now to tell you that I love you, too? I didn't want to freak you out, Andie, but it's been really difficult *not* to say it."

My heart tripped as I answered, "Yes. You don't have to say it unless it's true. I didn't blurt that out so that you'd reciprocate. I just . . . had to say it. I guess I was worried about telling you that too soon, but I've felt it, Noah." I put my free hand to my chest. "You're right here."

He leaned back against his pillow. "I promised I'd give you time, Andie—"

"I don't need it," I interrupted. "How often is someone like you going to come along for me? When am I ever going to feel this way again? It was stupid for me to keep hesitating. I *know* what I want. I want you. You were right when you said tomorrow is never guaranteed. You scared the shit out of me tonight. So I'm not holding back anymore, Noah. I hope you're ready for that."

He grinned. "When it comes to you, I'm ready for anything and everything you want to give me."

I smiled at him as I wiped away the last of my tears. "Right now, I just want to take care of you and make sure you get healthy again. Are you going to kick me out like you did your family if I fuss over you?"

"Nah. *You* can lecture me all you want."

I snorted. "Like you'd pay attention?"

"I'll hang on every word if it means you'll stick around."

Oh, he had *no idea* how much I was planning to stick around. I wasn't letting him out of my sight until he had recovered.

"I'm not going anywhere. It's not possible for you to scare me away, even if you do get grumpy." I was done thinking that I might not have a future. I'd gotten used to the idea that I didn't have to fret over that all the time anymore.

"I hate being in the hospital when I'm not really sick," he complained.

I rolled my eyes. "You're a terrible patient, and you're here for a reason. You have a concussion. Do you remember losing consciousness?"

He nodded. "I wasn't out for that long, but Aiden said it was a couple of minutes. All I remember is the sound of crunching metal, and then nothing until Aiden started screaming at me to wake up."

"He scared the crap out of me." Aiden's voice sounded near the door.

I turned and saw Owen wheeling Aiden into the room, with Skye trailing behind him.

"You okay?" Noah asked his brother sharply.

"Better than you, I think," Aiden answered drily. "I'm not the one lying in a hospital bed. I'm on my way home."

"Lucky bastard," Noah grumbled.

"I just wanted to see for myself that you're alert and talking. You took years off my life when you wouldn't open your damn eyes after the accident." Aiden was scanning Noah, his expression tense.

Noah waved his hand. "I'm alive. Go home and take care of yourself."

I had to bite back a smile. Noah was still issuing orders to his siblings, even from a hospital bed.

Maybe he had come a long way, but some of his habits and instincts were probably *never* going to change.

"*I'll* be taking care of him," Skye corrected. "It's going to take me a while to get over that phone call, and the frantic rush to the hospital in a panic."

"It was pretty nerve-wracking," Owen agreed. "Andie, do you want me to take you home?"

It took me a second to remember that I'd ridden here with Owen. "I don't have my car," I answered absently. "Honestly, I really want to stay here with Noah. Do you think they'd let me?"

I wasn't married to him, and I wasn't related. And he was in the ICU.

I didn't want to go anywhere. After what had happened, I'd be happy to just watch him sleep.

Owen nodded at the recliner I was perched on. "That chair will lie down flat so you can sleep. I'll get you something to sleep in and some blankets and pillows. The staff doesn't know me yet, and I'm not Noah's doctor, thank God. But I am a staff physician now, so I'll talk to them. I can get Seth to help me drop off your car in the morning."

I pulled my keys out of my purse and gave them to him. "Thank you."

"I'm taking Aiden home," Skye said firmly. "We'll call you in the morning, Noah."

I saw a speaking glance pass between Aiden and Noah, but I wasn't quite sure what they were saying without talking.

If I had to guess, I would have said that they were both counting their blessings in some way.

"You don't have to stay here, baby," Noah said in a low baritone. "Nothing is going to happen."

"I know," I said thoughtfully. "I *want* to be here with you. You'd feel the same way. Don't try to tell me you wouldn't."

If our positions were reversed, he wouldn't leave my room.

"I'd stay," he admitted grudgingly.

I beamed at him, shoved the chair flush with the bed, and piled the blankets and pillows on top of it when Owen brought them in.

"I'll see you both in the morning," he said as he handed me a pair of scrubs to sleep in.

I threw myself into Owen's arms and hugged him. "Thank you for coming to get me."

He was hugging me back when Noah said irritably, "Enough, already. Let go of my girl."

Owen winked at me, and I could tell he was amused as he let me go. "I was around long before you were," he said to antagonize his older brother.

"Yeah, which means you've had your chance already," Noah informed him. "Now get lost."

Owen chuckled as he exited the room and left the two of us alone.

The nurse came in to give Noah some pain medication, and I slipped into the bathroom to change into the roomy scrubs.

He was alone when I came back into the room. His nurse had shut off the overhead light, and there was only the dim illumination from a small light over the bed.

"I'll be right here if you need me. Sleep, Noah," I coaxed as I climbed into the recliner.

I put my feet up and my head down, but not low enough that I couldn't see him. I was exhausted now that my adrenaline wasn't pumping as hard, but I knew I wouldn't fall asleep anytime soon.

He reached down and put his hand over mine. I threaded my fingers through his and sighed.

"Thanks for staying," he said huskily.

I smiled into the darkness. "I warned you. If you want me out of your life, you're going to have to blast me out of it."

"Not going to happen. That week you didn't talk to me was the worst seven days of my life."

"Mine, too," I confessed.

Maybe I hadn't known him then as well as I did now, but the feelings had still been there, and the loss I'd felt when we'd parted had been profound.

I was quiet for a moment, and I heard Noah's breathing even out. Apparently, with the pain medication taking effect, he *was* going to be able to sleep.

CHAPTER 25

ANDIE

"I don't know how you did it, Andie. How can anyone stand to be in a hospital for as long as you were in for your leukemia?" Noah asked a week later.

I'd spent the whole week with him, working from his house and spending the nights in his bed.

He'd blown off the notion of me sleeping anywhere else, but he'd been so sore that nothing had happened, even though we *were* technically sleeping together.

I took a sip of my coffee. Noah and I had just sat down in the living room after eating takeout for dinner. He'd passed up the coffee and grabbed himself a beer.

I was careful not to press against him too hard as I leaned into him while we sat on the sofa.

I thought about his question for a moment before I answered. "I was really too sick to care. I guess it just became a way of life after a while."

"Do you mind talking about it?" he asked.

Usually, I refused to even *think* about that period of my life. "No," I answered him truthfully. For some reason, I didn't mind talking about it with him.

I was beginning to see it as a part of my past, and not my future.

"That first year . . ." His voice trailed off as if he didn't know what to say.

"It was a nightmare," I confessed. "I was looking at the reality of death every single day. I thought about all the things I'd never get to do before I was gone. I'd never travel. I'd never get married. I'd never have a child."

His arms tightened around me. "You were barely an adult. I can't even imagine what that would be like at the age of twenty."

"The second year was easier because I was steadily improving," I explained. "It almost seemed surreal when I was allowed to go back to my own apartment. I'd forgotten what a real, comfortable bed felt like. That year, I really wanted out of the hospital. Once I felt better, I was incredibly bored, but I spent a lot of time imagining the places I could go."

"Have you hit every place you dreamed about?"

"Pretty much," I answered. "There are more places I'd like to go, but I've gone to the ones high on my bucket list. It's been nice to just be home a while."

He kissed the top of my head. "I hate thinking about you being alone in the hospital."

"I had Owen," I reminded him. "And I would have been poor company for anyone else."

"What were the checkups like? You obviously had to be in Boston for them."

"They were stressful," I confessed. "I had to go in every month for a while, and then it stretched out to three months. Then it was six months. It's nice to know I won't have to see Boston for a year now. After next year, if everything looks good, I won't have to go again. I was scared for the first couple years, when I went to see my doctors often. I was terrified the cancer would come back."

"Did it get any better?"

I nodded. "I was still worried, but I didn't think about it every waking moment. I occupied myself with traveling, and only got really uneasy right before an exam."

"I'll be there with you next year," he said hoarsely as he played with my bracelets absently.

"I'm not going to let it rule my life anymore, Noah. I've learned my lesson. Anything can happen to anybody at any time. Your accident brought that point home. I want to live my life to the fullest every single day, and not worry about something that will probably never happen."

Does he still want to marry me? God, I hope so.

I was more than willing to commit.

If anything, seeing Noah in the hospital urged me not to squander a single moment that we had together.

There wasn't a single dark cloud on the horizon, and I wanted to go full speed ahead. In fact, I was looking forward to that.

I hoped I always lived in the moment, but I wanted to make plans for my future with Noah, too.

"I want you to move in with me. Is it too soon for that?" he asked hopefully.

I toyed with the buttons on his polo shirt. "I think I'm already living here."

Eventually, Noah and I would probably start working longer hours, and it would be nice if we lived in the same place.

"I mean permanently."

"I'm down with that. As long as you help me move," I teased.

"I'll have a moving truck at your place tomorrow," he offered.

I snorted. "Can you give me a few days to pack up?"

"No," he said high-handedly. "Now that you've agreed, I don't want you to have time to change your mind. There are plenty of rooms here that you can make into an office and more that you can use as your yoga and meditation room."

Noah had a huge home gym, and enough space there for my yoga and meditation area.

"Let's talk about it once you're completely healed," I suggested. "In the meantime, I'll be here."

"I am healed, Andie," he said stubbornly.

I rolled my eyes. "You're still bruised up."

"They're painless now."

I didn't believe him. Maybe he *wasn't* in much pain anymore, but I highly doubted he was pain-free. "Let's get into the hot tub."

We'd been using the Jacuzzi every night to help ease his soreness.

I jumped up, and Noah rose a moment later. "Are you trying to change the subject, Andie?"

"Not at all. I'm just trying to get you to be reasonable."

He pulled off his shirt and tossed it onto the couch. He'd thought ahead and was already wearing a pair of swim trunks.

"I'm never unreasonable," he said as he walked toward the sliding doors. "What do I have to do to prove that I'm one hundred percent healthy?"

Okay. Fine.

Then I was going to see just how healthy he was. There was still a nagging distance between the two of us because we hadn't become intimate again, and I was about to see if I could breach it.

He still had some bruises to his rib area, but those contusions *were* fading.

Maybe he *was* capable of doing *anything*.

I followed him outside and watched as he turned on the hot tub.

"Aren't you coming?" he asked, raising a brow in question.

"I plan on it," I said in a sensual tone that I almost didn't recognize. I hadn't used it since the time I'd been in Mexico with him.

Do it, Andie. Take the plunge.

Noah was healing, and there was nothing I wanted more than to indulge in every kind of sensual pleasure I could imagine.

We might have to adjust or stop if his movements were painful, but I wanted that connection back, and I was determined to jump-start that part of our relationship again.

I couldn't go another day without touching him the way I wanted.

If he was still too hesitant to make a move, then *I'd* make one.

I'd been the one to put that distance between us in the first place, and I was ready to break down that wall.

He entered the bubbling water and then turned to face me.

Grabbing the hem of my shirt, I jerked it over my head and dropped it on the cement.

"Andie? Are you going to change?" Noah's voice sounded raspy.

I met his eyes and held his stare. "I love to get into a hot tub naked," I told him as I slowly unclipped the front fastening of my bra.

His eyes flared with heat, and that urged me on. I let the flimsy piece of lingerie fall down my arms and I shook it off.

Noah's expression was hungry and fierce as he looked at me with a primal longing that shook me to my core.

"I'm not going to argue," he said, his voice harsh. "Feel free to get as naked as you want."

I shot him a sultry smile as I reached for the button on my denim shorts. "Thanks. I definitely will."

He was watching me like a predator now, and I reveled in the heat I saw in his expression.

The desire.

The passion.

The need.

The longing.

God, I could feel all of those things myself, and it was consuming me.

"I'm tired of waiting, Noah. I can't do it anymore. I want you too much. I love you too much," I explained to him as I flipped the button and then lowered the zipper.

"You can never love me too much. I was tired of waiting weeks ago," he agreed gutturally. "I just didn't want to rush you."

"You're not rushing me. I think I'm going to end up seducing *you*."

"You're doing a damn good job of it so far," he answered, staring at me like he was mesmerized.

I wiggled my hips and pulled the jean shorts and my panties down my legs, and then kicked them off.

"Come over here," he growled as he started to get up from his seat in the tub.

"So bossy," I murmured as I sauntered over to the in-ground tub and slowly made my way down the cement steps. "Do you always get what you want?"

He stood and wrapped his arms around me the second my foot hit the bottom of the stairs. "Hardly ever," he said in a throaty tone. "But I'm going to *this time*."

I looked up at him in the dim light of the patio. God, he was magnificent. He was staring at me like he wanted to devour me whole, and his eyes radiated a hot promise that made my core clench with anticipation.

I put my hands on his muscular shoulders. "I'm all yours."

CHAPTER 26

Andie

"Do you have any idea how long I've waited for you to say those words? That you belong to me?" Noah said in a rough voice.

"I love you," I told him as I put my arms around his neck. "I think you're my reward for getting through everything that's gone wrong for me so far."

He grumbled, "I love you, sweetheart, but I doubt I'm any woman's prize."

I shook my head. "You're mine," I disagreed. "You're the one thing in my life that has gone right. I don't want to ruin us. I should have told you I loved you. I should have seen what's so damn clear right in front of my face. I should have jumped at the chance to marry you. And I should have never let you put any barriers between us physically, when all I wanted was for you to fuck me senseless. I want you, Noah. It's only ever been you."

Deep in my soul, I knew I'd been waiting for this man so I could give him all of me.

He threaded his hands in my hair and tilted my head up. "There's no going back after this, Andie," he said thickly. "I can't do it."

I shivered as I held his gaze.

I wanted Noah to know that I was *never* going back. That he wouldn't have to hold back for me. Not anymore. "No going back. All I want is our future, whatever it might hold."

He fisted my hair. "There is no damn future for me without you in it."

I swallowed hard as I fell into his intense hazel-eyed gaze. Noah was my everything, so I knew exactly how he felt. "I'll be here," I said with a certainty I'd never completely felt until recently.

"Damn right you will," he answered rigidly as his head swooped down to kiss me.

The possession in his embrace made me crazy.

I opened for him so his marauding tongue could sweep inside my mouth, and I shuddered with pleasure.

Every painful ache of desire I'd felt was temporarily softened by the way this man could brand me with a single kiss.

I put all of my frustrations, all of my joy, all of my happiness into kissing him back. I needed Noah to understand that I wanted every bit of his fierceness.

I yearned for him to take everything I was offering with a ferocity that was going to satisfy us both.

Heat and steam surrounded us, enfolded us, and it added to the potency of his erotic kiss.

His hands slicked down my back and landed on my ass as he pulled me tighter against his powerful body.

Yes. Yes. Yes.

I could feel his thick cock straining against the material of his suit, and I moaned as he lifted his head.

I clawed at the cotton material, dying to get him as naked as I was. "Fuck me," I begged, panting with the need to get him inside me.

We'd waited too damn long.

I wasn't willing to wait another second.

I yanked the suit to his ankles, and he stepped out of it as his mouth explored the sensitive skin of my neck.

Tossing the suit, I didn't even look to see where it was going to land. I didn't give a damn as long as it wasn't obstructing the feel of Noah's bare skin against mine.

My head fell back to give him access to anything he wanted, and I braced myself by stretching my arms out to lie along the cemented sides of the hot tub.

"Noah," I said in a breathless voice, wallowing in the feel of his mouth devouring every bare inch of skin he could find. "I need you."

This man overwhelmed me.

He exposed me.

And then, he sheltered me.

I trembled as his tongue flicked over one of my hardened nipples.

I squeaked when his teeth nipped at the vulnerable tip.

There was a second of pain, and then sweet relief as his tongue circled and laved over the exact spot where he'd just pinched with his teeth.

It felt so damn good, so sensual and arousing that it was almost hard to bear.

"I need you inside me, Noah," I demanded.

"You'll have to wait," he ground out right before he took my nipple between his fingers and squeezed.

He was tormenting me, taking complete control, and if I hadn't had support from the side of the tub, my knees would have buckled.

Oh, God. "Why?"

He rose up and speared me with a stare that was nothing but naked desire and hot, carnal sensuality. "Because you're going to want me to fuck you just as much as I want to bury myself inside you."

"I do," I whimpered.

"No, I don't think that you do," he said roughly as his hand stroked up one of my thighs. He was met by a scorching, thick liquid heat that hadn't been washed away by the water. "You're wet for me," he growled.

My eyes nearly rolled back in my head when he slid through my folds and fondled the sensitive, pink flesh of my pussy.

His finger found my clit, and stroked over it as he leaned in and growled beside my ear, "This is mine, Andie. It's always going to be mine."

"Always," I repeated eagerly as I pushed my hips against that tantalizing touch. "Please, Noah. I need you."

"Tell me how much," he demanded. "Tell me what you need."

I was shaking with the urgency to climax, but he was holding me on the edge.

I could feel his heated breath wafting over my ear, and the sensual feel of the hot water lapping against my skin.

Every nerve in my body was so hypersensitive that every sensation was putting me into overload.

"I-need-you-to-fuck-me." If he didn't, I was going to lose my mind.

"Not yet," he drawled in a low voice that vibrated against my ear. "Come for me, Andie."

My back arched as Noah increased the pressure on the swollen, engorged bundle of nerves, and I felt like my body was being pulled apart.

"Noah!" I cried out. "Please fuck me!"

I couldn't take much more.

I was suffused with a powerful craving I'd never experienced before. For Noah.

For satisfaction.

For a relief from the pounding desire that I couldn't survive anymore.

"Come for me, baby," he demanded in a voice that I'd never heard from him before.

"I'm going to get you for this later," I screamed at him.

I loved and hated his dominance.

Fortunately, I adored it more than I wanted to get away.

"I look forward to it," he answered cockily as he ground his palm into my pussy, slamming me with exactly the force I needed to let go.

My orgasm hit me like a racing vehicle, fast and full throttle.

"Yes!" I moaned, that one word all I could manage as I was buffeted by the forceful climax.

I wrapped my arms around his powerful shoulders as I floated back to earth.

I nipped his earlobe in playful retribution, and then rested my head on his shoulder as I wrapped my legs around his waist. "I need you inside me, Noah. No more messing around."

I was more than primed; I was desperate now.

Rather than being satisfied by my orgasm, it had just made me hungrier for him, and I was pretty sure he knew it.

He wanted me this way.

He needed me this way.

I could sense it.

"Fuck. Me." I bit his earlobe, and I felt his body vibrate with hunger as I fisted my hands in his hair. "Now."

He gripped my hair and his mouth crashed down on mine.

Our tongues dueled, sliding together exactly like I wanted our entire bodies fused. When he finally lifted his head, we were both panting with need.

He nibbled at my bottom lip, and then licked the tiny hurt before he kissed me full force one more time.

"Not. Here," he rasped when he released my lips.

Noah put his hands on my ass and lifted me.

My legs wrapped tight around his waist as he stood and walked us both out of the water.

"Noah. Stop. You were hurt—"

"Do you think that I even notice that right now?" he grunted. "The only thing I can think about right now is burying myself to the balls inside you."

"Yes! Yes! Yes!"

I wanted that more than I could express, but I didn't want him to kill himself to do it.

"Where are we going?" Our bodies were trailing water across the brick pavers as he strode to the patio door.

"Exactly where I've wanted you for weeks," he said in a deep, ardent tone as he jerked open the slider and then slammed it closed behind us.

"Naked. And. In. My. Bed."

CHAPTER 27

ANDIE

I was already a mass of aching need and hungry desire, so I thought it would be impossible for it to quicken even more. But it did. The second he'd uttered those five little possessive words.

"Naked. And. In. My. Bed."

Hell, yes. I'd slept there every night for a week, wondering what it would be like if Noah and I were setting his sheets on fire.

Now, after all that torment, I was finally going to find out.

Noah had an elevator to the upper floor, but he bypassed it. "Too damn slow," he muttered as he mounted the stairs and pounded up them, our bodies still flinging off some droplets of water as he traversed the steps in record time.

"We're wet," I squealed as he entered his room and yanked back the covers on the bed.

He tossed me onto the fitted sheet. "I want you wet," he grumbled, deliberately being obtuse.

I stared up at him with a desperate yearning as he just looked at me. He seemed to be taking stock of exactly how I appeared naked and wet in his bed.

"Fucking fantastic," he said roughly. "Better than a damn wet dream."

Wet dream?

I wanted to ask him if he had as many erotic dreams about me as I had about him, but I never got the chance.

He was on me in the next heartbeat, kissing me, touching me, and my body went up in flames.

Noah rolled me on top of him. "Ride me, woman," he demanded. "Take me inside that gorgeous body of yours and put me out of my misery."

It was both a command and a plea, and there was no way I was going to refuse.

I let my legs fall to his sides as every wild instinct I'd ever had took control. "No misery," I said to him softly as I grasped his hard cock and put it exactly where I wanted. "Just you and me. Just pleasure."

I relished the hunger in his eyes as I lowered myself down on him. I took his length and girth slowly, inch by inch, savoring the way he fit inside me like a glove.

"God, you're perfect," I moaned as his cock became fully encased inside me.

"Fuck!" Noah cursed in a raspy voice. "You're killing me, Andie."

I placed my palms on his shoulders, avoiding the areas where he'd been hurt. "I'll bring you back to life," I promised with a gasp.

"Take what you want, baby," he ordered. "I want to watch you."

His request should have made me uncomfortable. After all, I wasn't exactly that experienced. But it shot right through me, setting me on fire in a matter of moments.

Nothing pleased him more than watching me. I already knew that.

I lifted myself and slid Noah's cock almost out, and then sank back down while he filled me again.

And then I kept doing it because it felt so good.

"Jesus Christ!" Noah cursed as he grasped my hips. "You're the hottest woman I've ever known. I want you so damn bad I'm not sure if I can make this last. But I want to."

I sat up and put my head back. I could feel him watching me as he held my hips and thrust up, coming upward in a powerful surge.

Over and over.

Faster and faster.

I felt taken, and the relief of that was so amazing that I could already feel my climax building.

"Fuck me," I moaned, grinding down each time he pummeled inside me.

I reached for oblivion, and it found me in the slapping of our skin coming together, and the wild, carnal motion of our bodies.

"Noah!" I cried out, almost frightened by the intensity of the emotions welling up inside me.

He reached up and supported me as he rolled until he was on top of me, his body covering mine. Noah never missed a beat as he kept up a punishing rhythm, his cock pounding inside me like he couldn't and wouldn't ever stop.

I wrapped my legs tightly around him, needing him closer.

The feel of his damp, hot, naked skin sliding against mine was agonizingly sweet.

I felt . . . completely consumed.

I couldn't get enough of him.

My fingernails dug into his back as I tried to climb inside his soul.

"You're mine, Andie," he growled as he reached underneath me and grabbed my ass with one hand, trying to tilt my hips so he could go a little bit deeper. "You'll always be mine."

He was going to be mine, too. Forever. I felt that knowledge deep inside my being.

My orgasm was rolling toward me, and I couldn't answer. I bit down on his shoulder, trying to show him that I wasn't going anywhere.

"Fuck, yeah," he groaned, like he reveled in the fact that I'd just claimed him as mine without a single word.

I exploded into the carnality of our fierce joining, my heart soaring as my body shook with the force of my release.

"Noah! I love you!" I screamed with abandon.

My walls spasmed and clamped down hard on his cock.

"Love you, too, baby. So. Damn. Much." His voice was harsh, and he groaned as I milked him to his own hot release.

He rolled off me and jerked me to his side as we recovered, both of us huffing to find our breath.

After we'd recovered, I had no desire to move. Noah and I were cocooned together, and I sighed happily as he murmured words of love and adoration next to my ear.

I was at peace in a way I hadn't ever been before, and it was all because of the gloriously naked man who was holding me, showing me how much I meant to him.

"I don't want to get up," I confessed. "But the bed is wet."

"Then we'll just find another one," he muttered as he nuzzled the side of my neck. "I have plenty of them in this house."

I snorted. "Are you planning on trying every bed in this place?"

"If that's what it takes to keep you in one," he agreed.

I turned to him and wrapped my arms around his neck. "I think I probably need to shower first. I still have the chemicals from the hot tub all over me."

"I'd be up for that," he muttered. "Literally."

I laughed. Noah was a strong, virile guy, and I had no doubt he could rise to the occasion. "You just got beat up in a car accident a week ago," I reminded him playfully.

"And I've been waiting to get you naked for weeks," he said earnestly. "Which one do you think takes priority?"

"Aren't you sore? You just picked me up and lugged me up a flight of stairs, and then got a serious workout."

He combed my hair absently with his fingers. "I'm too damn happy to feel any pain."

I sighed. "Why did you wait so long? If I hadn't seduced you, how long were you planning to keep us in a state of frustration?"

"It's been hell," he admitted. "But I didn't want to screw everything up by pushing you into bed too soon. You're too important to me, Andie. I knew damn well that the minute you decided to get intimate, I was done pretending that I could wait to call you mine."

"Were you pretending?" I asked curiously.

"My feelings never changed," he said hoarsely. "So yeah, it was a pretense in that sense. My end goal was to have you fully committed. Heart, mind, soul, and body. I was willing to do whatever I had to do to achieve that. But I can tell you that I wasn't going to wait much longer. It was killing me."

I'd never been a real believer in insta-lust or insta-love, but I'd probably fallen for Noah soon after I'd seen him on that jet, his head in his computer, a frantic expression on his handsome face.

I'm not sure how things would have gone had I never had leukemia, and never been terrified of long-term commitments. I wasn't entirely sure we wouldn't be married already.

"You didn't have to wait," I told him. "I've been crazy about you since day one, Noah. I learned my lesson as soon as we spent that week apart from each other. I wanted to dive in headfirst, but I was still scared. None of my hesitation was ever about you, or the way I felt about you."

"I know," he said huskily. "I just wanted you to be sure. I'm so damn in love with you that I can't even stand thinking about you not being there with me in the future."

"No fear," I said in a coaxing voice. "Not anymore. I want to live every single day with you like it's my last, even if it's not."

My heart swelled with love for the man who had been willing to wait, willing to be stubbornly persistent until I was ready.

"Me too, sweetheart," he responded.

I stroked a hand over his hair. "Nobody has ever loved me like you do," I said wistfully.

"Ditto," he said gutturally. "I know my family loves me, but it isn't the same. They don't see me like you do."

I smiled at him because I knew he could really see me, too.

In some ways, I wished *everyone* could see the inherent kindness in Noah, the goodness inside his heart.

Then again, I liked being the only one who could really peer inside his soul.

He rolled out of bed and held out his hand. "Shower time, woman."

"Now?"

He nodded. "Right now. I don't think I can wait another second."

I scanned his gorgeous body and face, and my eyes stopped when I got to his completely erect cock.

My body shuddered in reaction. "Take me away." I put my hand in his.

He pulled me up and swept me into his arms.

I gasped in reaction, but I didn't even try to argue as I wrapped my arms around his neck.

This amazing, beautiful, sexy man was free to take me anywhere he wanted to go.

I'd waited way too long for him to protest now.

CHAPTER 28

Noah

A few days later, I watched Andie as she played with my niece, Maya, in the backyard of Aiden's home.

Skye had decided it was time to get the family together now that Aiden and I had recovered from our injuries, and Andie had heartily agreed.

"She looks happy," Aiden observed from his seat right next to me.

Andie and I had arrived early, so we were the only guests there so far.

"I hope she is," I answered honestly.

"You look pretty damn elated yourself. I take it you've gotten over the hump."

I knew Aiden was really asking if I'd gotten laid. "I think we got everything resolved. Now I just have to figure out how to ask her to marry me."

Since Andie was ready to walk into the future together, I wanted to put a ring on her finger as soon as possible. I wasn't about to wonder whether it was too soon to make that move.

Andie said she was over her fear, and I had to believe that she was.

"Whoa," Aiden said, lifting a brow as he looked at me. "I didn't know we were looking at a wedding that soon. We just got Seth married off."

"I hope you bought your tux," I told him. "You're going to need it."

"I didn't," he said drily. "But I'll be more than happy to get one."

"I'm not sure I want the big wedding. All I want is to be married to Andie. I don't need all that other stuff, and I'm not sure she's going to want it, either."

She was a roll-with-the-flow type of woman, and somehow, I just couldn't see her being happy with all the fuss.

"I think she'd take the honeymoon, though," I said thoughtfully. "I'd have to find a unique place to take her, somewhere she hasn't been before."

"You find yourself a jet?" Aiden questioned.

"As a matter of fact, I did. Andie helped me. We're looking forward to breaking it in."

"What about kids?" he asked.

I shrugged. Although I'd love to see Andie pregnant with my child, I was ambivalent about having children. "I could go either way, so I'll let Andie decide. If she wants them, she'll get them when she's ready."

Aiden took a slug of the beer he was holding, his eyes on something near where the women were being entertained by my niece. "Who's that?" he asked.

I followed his gaze to see Andie enthusiastically hugging a new female arrival. "That's Layla. She hung out a lot with Owen and Andie when they were younger. She's a nurse practitioner at Owen's new practice. Andie asked Skye if she could invite her. I hope you don't mind."

"Nah. The more the merrier," Aiden answered. "I just didn't recognize her. She grew up."

We'd all seen Layla when she was younger, but it had been a long time. "She's nice. But Andie mentioned that Layla and Owen aren't really getting along. I'm not sure why. The only reason she came today is because Owen *isn't* coming."

"He is coming," Aiden informed me.

"He told me he wasn't." I'd spoken to my youngest brother earlier, and he'd insisted that he was too busy to make it today.

"Owen texted me just a few minutes ago and said he'd finished moving into his new place earlier than he thought, and that he'd stop by. He's probably coming so he doesn't have to cook," Aiden joked.

Obviously, Layla and Andie didn't know about Owen's change of plan. "That could be awkward."

"Is she single?"

I nodded. "Yeah."

"Maybe you should offer her the opportunity to participate in the beta for your dating app," he suggested.

I leaned back in my chair. "I just might do that. *You're* certainly no help."

Aiden chuckled. "I don't think Skye wants me to make a profile, and I know I sure as hell don't want her posting her picture there."

"I didn't give it to Andie, either," I confessed. "Not that I don't trust *her*, but I don't have any faith in all the men out there."

"I know exactly what you mean," Aiden agreed.

"I don't know if I should give Layla the beta. There's so many people doing the beta right now."

"Is Owen doing it?" Aiden questioned, his tone curious.

"Yeah. I gave it to him. He's the only unattached brother I have left."

"He'll end up swamped with inquiries. I hope he uses a fake profile. He's rich, and he's a doctor."

"I told him to try to hide his identity. He doesn't have to tell anyone unless he actually wants to meet up with somebody."

Aiden was quiet for a minute before he said, "It seems like something is up with him. I thought he'd be really happy that his med school and residency were finally over. But he doesn't exactly seem elated. Do you think he's missing Boston?"

I shook my head. "I don't think so. He said he missed Citrus Beach and the California weather, but I noticed that he's been pretty quiet. I have no idea what's on his mind. He hasn't really talked to me about it, if he's having problems adjusting."

"Me either. It's not like he seems miserable. He just doesn't seem . . . normal. He's always been the most studious and quiet one in the family, but he's not as excited about buying Dr. Fortney's practice as I expected. Maybe it's just because he's been pretty busy. He's still getting settled, and he's already working in a practice. Plus, he just bought a new house."

My little brother did have a lot on his plate. "I guess we wait and see if things change now that he's moved into his place. Maybe he's just preoccupied."

"Do you think we should tell Layla that Owen is coming? He said he wouldn't be here until later."

"I wouldn't. The ladies look like they're having a good time. It would be a shame if she left just because Owen was coming. She *does* work with him every day." It wasn't like Layla could just walk away from Owen when she was in the office.

I watched as Andie shot Layla a happy grin, and my chest ached just from seeing her smile.

I'd seen that smile directed at me.

And it hit me right in the gut every single time.

I wanted to go snap her up and carry her back home so I could get her naked.

I'd been surprised when she'd stripped and offered herself up to me a few days ago. Not that it wasn't a welcome shock. In fact, if she hadn't seduced me, I wouldn't have lasted much longer.

I'd been on the edge of sanity, and ready to fall off the cliff, when she'd saved me by being brave enough to make the first move.

"I love her," I muttered as I stared at her.

"I hope so," Aiden said wryly. "If you don't, it probably isn't wise to be talking about pledging the rest of your life to her."

I shot him a dirty look. I hadn't meant to say those words out loud. They'd just tumbled from my mouth before I could stop them.

"Smartass," I rumbled.

Aiden grinned. "In all seriousness, I'm glad everything worked out."

Oh, hell, it *had* to work out. I'd be useless if it didn't. "Thanks."

"Should we go join the ladies?" Aiden asked.

We might as well, because I couldn't stop looking their way.

"I think we should," I said as I stood.

Aiden smirked. "You've got it bad, bro."

"Are you trying to tell me that you aren't dying to go be with Skye?" I knew damn well he couldn't wait to be closer to his wife and child.

"Nope," Aiden admitted as he stood up. "I'm just saying that now you're in the same boat as me, Seth, Eli, and Liam."

I grinned at him. That was one group I didn't mind signing up for at all. "I'm glad that boat has room for one more."

CHAPTER 29

OWEN

I was going to be late getting to Aiden's family gathering, and I was starving, so I was hoping he still had food.

I increased my pace, walking faster down the beach as I remembered exactly how much food my family could put down in one night.

Seth and Aiden alone could eat more than a half-dozen people put together could.

Since my new home wasn't far from Aiden's, it was easier to just walk it by shortcutting down the beach.

I'd been busy unpacking the things I'd ordered for my new home, and I'd kind of lost track of time.

Almost settled. I had most of what I needed in the house. Now, if I could manage to make it look like home.

The new place was huge, a hell of a lot bigger than I needed. But I figured I'd grow into it. I might get married someday. Have kids. Actually have some kind of life.

After years of nothing but medical school dominating my entire existence in Boston, I wasn't quite used to having my own home, and being back in Citrus Beach again.

I was a damn billionaire.

I had my own practice now.

I had a huge house on the water.

I had my family close again.

And I had absolutely no idea how to live in my new lifestyle.

Not that I didn't like being back with my family. I'd missed all of them. It just seemed strange that they were close physically, and that I could just walk over and talk to them when I wanted.

And the billionaire thing? *Inconceivable.*

Who wouldn't want to be in possession of one of the biggest fortunes in the world? The problem was getting used to it after counting every penny I had during med school and my residency.

I could do anything I wanted to do.

I could buy anything I wanted.

I'd definitely taken the rich-guy thing for a spin when I'd purchased my house, the contents, and a new vehicle.

Problem was, I still felt like a poor resident.

Yeah, I certainly wasn't complaining about the ability to sit down and pay off every bill I had, including a ton of student debt.

I just wasn't used to seeing something I liked and realizing that I actually had the power to buy it without putting even a tiny dent into the money I'd inherited.

Being a rich man had never been a big priority for me. A family physician made decent money, but even with all of the help from my siblings, I'd still managed to acquire quite a bit of debt in student loans, so I'd known I wouldn't exactly be living the high life once my residency was over.

The money I'd make being a doctor was never a consideration when I'd chosen a career path.

All I'd ever wanted was to put my brain to work on treating medical problems.

I have my own practice now.

I shook my head as I continued walking. I guessed I'd known my training was leading to all of this.

It was just weird to be *living* the life I'd worked for in the last decade.

Dr. Fortney retiring just as I was finishing my residency had been a happy coincidence.

Perfect.

The best thing that could have ever happened, considering I'd wanted to get back to Citrus Beach.

There was only one downside, and it came in the form of one incredibly gorgeous, wickedly smart, and highly disgruntled nurse practitioner.

I'd inherited Layla. She'd been part of the package. Dr. Fortney had called her one of his greatest assets.

I called her a huge pain in the ass.

The woman didn't like me, even though we'd been close at one time. Somewhere near the end of our senior year in high school, Layla had changed. She'd blown me off like I'd never existed. If she'd carried around some acrimony, she should have gotten over it a long time ago.

It was high school, for God's sake.

Andie had mentioned that Layla and I were too competitive, but I'd never felt that way toward Layla.

I'll give it some time. Maybe it will all work out.

I'd only seen Layla a couple of times, since the transition of the practice from Dr. Fortney to me had just been completed.

We'd discussed a couple of cases, and Layla had treated me like a stranger. No, she'd been colder than that. More like an opponent who she was forced to get along with, or she'd get kicked out of a game.

Why was I letting her get to me?

Maybe because I'd been so stunned the first time I saw her again.

Layla had grown into a drop-dead-gorgeous woman. As a kid, she'd lacked confidence, even though she'd had no reason to be self-conscious.

She had grown into her intelligence, and now she carried herself like a woman who knew exactly what she had going for herself.

I hated myself because I was attracted to her, even though I knew I shouldn't be.

Layla was a professional woman, an associate, and technically, I was her boss now.

Unfortunately, I had all I could do not to imagine her naked, looking at me like she wanted . . . me.

"Fuck!" I cursed out loud.

Not going to happen. She wasn't going to let me get her naked. Hell, I couldn't get within five feet of her without her freezing solid.

I think I just need to get laid.

Yeah, that was probably the issue.

Layla was beautiful.

Confident.

Smart.

I hadn't ever really had sex on a regular basis, or a steady girlfriend.

Makes sense that I'm attracted to Layla, right?

I'd get over it.

I tried to shrug off my strange attraction to Layla as I entered the back gate to Aiden's house.

It took me all of two seconds to realize that it wasn't going to be that easy to rid myself of thoughts about Layla.

Not when the subject of my torment was standing five feet away from me.

What the hell is she doing here?

"Owen? What are you doing here?" Layla sounded surprised.

She was sitting all alone in a lounge chair. It looked like everybody else was in the pool.

"Me?" I asked cautiously. "Last time I checked, my brother lived here."

"Andie said you weren't coming."

Okay. Andie had invited her. It pissed me off that it sounded like she wouldn't have come if she'd known I was going to be here.

I put my hands in the pockets of my jeans. "Change of plan."

I didn't have to explain myself.

She stood. "I should get going, anyway."

"Why? Just because I'm here? I don't get it, Layla. It's not like we were never friends. We used to like being around each other." *What the hell happened?*

"That changed near the end of our senior year," she answered icily.

Yeah, something *had* altered between us, but I'd never really understood *why*.

"Yeah, about that . . . what in the hell happened? Why did you just throw away years of friendship? I don't get it."

She grabbed her purse from the lounge chair and fumbled for her keys. "You know why," she said stoically as she drew her keys from her bag. "Please don't try to make it out to be nothing."

To me, whatever her reason was for disliking me, it *was* nothing, because I couldn't remember doing a damn thing to make her want to ignore me.

I'd gone away to Boston still not understanding what had happened to make her change so much that last month of high school.

Honestly, I'd been more than a little hurt by her actions.

I'd talked to Andie about it, but she hadn't had a clue why Layla was acting so strange.

"Never mind," Layla said snippily. "It was a long time ago. It doesn't matter."

"Don't go, Layla," I said, wishing she'd stay.

To tell the truth, I'd missed her. Maybe I hadn't realized just how much until I'd seen her again.

Or maybe I'd blocked it out because there was nothing I could do about it in Boston, when she was back here in California.

She pinned me with a laser-sharp look. "I'll see you Monday in the office, Dr. Sinclair."

I stood in the middle of the patio as she sashayed toward the sliding doors and disappeared inside.

What. The. Hell.

It wasn't like I could run after her and demand she explain herself. Could I?

I shook my head as I realized that was *exactly* what I wanted to do.

I forced myself to stay put until I knew she was probably gone, and then I walked toward the grill to see if there was anything left to eat.

I absolutely refused to jog after her like we were still high-school kids, and beg her to tell me what was wrong.

Not that I was giving up on getting to the bottom of her animosity.

I'd just have to find a different way to get her to talk.

CHAPTER 30

ANDIE

"Where are we going?" I said, laughing as Noah gently nudged me up the steps of his new jet.

"I'll tell you once we're airborne," he answered, still not giving me any hints of where we'd end up on the maiden journey of his new aircraft.

Not that I really cared.

I'd go anywhere with this man who I loved.

I sighed as we arrived inside the plane. The basic layout was much like Eli Stone's, but the décor was very different.

Instead of a bar, Noah had installed an open yoga studio, with all of the accessories.

There was a comfy seating area with a sofa and chairs, and leather recliners for takeoff.

I slipped into my seat for takeoff, and Noah sat down next to me.

I breathed in and wallowed in the smell of new leather.

"It's amazing," I told him as I buckled my seat belt. "Thank you for thinking of me with the yoga area."

He shrugged once his belt was fastened. "I thought about you while they were planning out all of the décor. We'll be traveling a lot. I want you to be comfortable."

I let out a big sigh. There was rarely a time that Noah wasn't thinking about me being happy. How could I not love that about him?

"I'm still waiting for you to tell me where we're going."

He reached out and took my hand. "Just be still," he insisted.

I smiled. Noah had tried to learn yoga and meditation, but he'd never really been into it, which was perfectly fine with me.

However, he seemed to love to be still, especially when he didn't want to talk about something.

Okay, maybe that wasn't *completely* true.

He seemed to *enjoy* those periods of stillness, when we just sat together in the moment, but this one seemed particularly way too well timed.

I was quiet as we took off, just enjoying the kind of peace I could only find when I was with Noah.

When we were together, there was nothing else I wanted, nothing else I really needed.

My world, and everything in it, was perfect.

"You were serious when you said you'd be fine getting married without a big wedding, right?" Noah asked once we were in the air and reached our cruising altitude.

I swallowed hard. "Yes. But I'd never do that."

Noah and I had talked about marriage, and a possible wedding, but it had been hypothetical since he hadn't actually asked me to marry him yet.

I'd mentioned that I'd love to just elope, run away somewhere and get married since there would be nobody to sit on the bride's side of the aisle. My parents were never in Citrus Beach, and I doubted my mother would suddenly decide she wanted to be involved in my life by participating in wedding plans.

Of course, Noah's side would be overcrowded with all of his family.

I'd meant it as a joke. I would never deny Noah a proper wedding where all of his family could attend.

"Why not?" His tone was curious.

"Noah, your family would never forgive me. They'd all want to see you marry."

"This isn't about our family, Andie. It's about us." He unfastened his seat belt and got up, only to drop down in front of me.

My breath caught as he drew a red-velvet jewelry box from the pocket of his jeans. "I've been carrying this ring around for weeks. I kept waiting for the right time. I guess what I didn't realize was that it was always the right time because I had the right woman. I hope you're ready to take it."

He popped the box open.

Tears sprang to my eyes as I looked at the perfect, shockingly large diamond winking at me.

"Marry me, Andie. Put me out of my misery," Noah said huskily.

I laughed. The demand was so authentically Noah that I couldn't help myself.

I nodded as tears trickled down my cheeks. "It took you long enough."

He grinned up at me as he pulled the ring from the box and put it on my finger. "I wanted to make sure you'd say *yes*."

I doubted very much that he would have *ever* taken no for an answer, but my heart ached over the fact that Noah had given me time and space when he'd thought that I needed it.

He was completely unselfish in that way, and there were very few people who truly had that kind of thoughtfulness in their nature.

Luckily, I was going to marry a guy who would always put my needs before his own, even though I didn't want him to do it.

I'd never take him for granted, and I'd always put his needs before mine, too. I loved him too much *not* to do it.

"I love you," I said tearfully as I fumbled to undo my seat belt.

The second I was free, I threw myself into his arms.

"I love you, too, Andie," he said, his voice guttural as he wrapped his arms around me.

I hugged him tightly. "Thank you for waiting for me."

I'd hesitated once, but I'd never do it again.

Life and time were too damn precious to waste.

He sat back down in his recliner and pulled me into his lap. "I didn't know I was actually waiting until I met you."

I lowered my head and kissed him. It was a slow, thorough embrace of promise and tender devotion.

Putting my forehead against his once our lips had parted, I let out a shaky breath.

Noah had the power to love me or destroy me, but I had complete faith in him and his intentions.

"I'm taking you to Napa," he said in a casual tone.

I froze. "You're kidding, right?"

"Not kidding," he denied.

In the same conversation that I made that joke about eloping, I'd also said that I wished I could just quietly get married outside in a vineyard somewhere.

It had sounded so romantic, and so amazingly simple.

Certainly, he didn't think . . .

"Marry me there, Andie. Let's make it simple and beautiful. Just you and me. We'll make our promises together. Without all of the fuss."

"Noah, we can't. Your siblings and cousins—"

"Will survive just fine without another damn wedding to attend," he finished. "When we get back to California, we can have a big damn party with an enormous cake, and a bunch of great food. After that, we'll figure out where we want to go on our honeymoon."

God, I was so down with what he was proposing.

A simple ceremony in a vineyard.

A romantic dinner and a stroll through the rolling hills after it was over.

No crazy wedding frenzies.

No frantic preparations.

No uneven sides of the aisle.

I knew damn well Noah was doing this for me. "Is this *really* what you want?"

"Yeah," he answered, sounding truthful. "There's been plenty of weddings in my family. All I want is to be married to you, Andie. I want to stand face to face and make our vows. That's all that matters."

I was flustered. "I don't have a dress—"

"We'll shop. I'm not going to make you say your vows today. Or tomorrow. We have time to make everything perfect."

I put my head on his shoulder as my entire body started to shake.

Within seconds, I was wracked with big, ugly sobs that I couldn't hold back.

Noah put his hand up and stroked over my hair gently. "Oh, fuck! Don't cry," he rasped, his tone worried.

"I can't help it. You shouldn't be so amazing, and I probably wouldn't cry," I choked out.

"Does that mean you're game for the plan?" He sounded incredibly hopeful.

"I'm all over it," I answered as I raised my head and swiped the tears from my face. Maybe what I'd said wasn't *completely* a joke.

It had actually been what I'd consider a perfect wedding.

I just hadn't admitted it to myself at the time.

But somehow, Noah had known, even when I hadn't.

"We definitely need to have that big party," I warned him. "I'd like to meet your East Coast family, and I wouldn't feel right if there wasn't some family celebration."

"I'm sure Riley, Skye, and Jade would be happy to help you plan it," he said drily.

"And Layla," I added.

"You can do that up any way you want," he offered. "As long as it has good food."

I punched him in the arm playfully. "I think that's my line."

He stood up, sweeping me up into his arms as he got out of his seat. "It's a short flight. I think we better hurry."

I gave him a questioning look. "Why?"

He opened the door to the bedroom, and tossed me onto the bed. "We need to break in this damn jet."

I snorted. "I think you mean we need to try out the bed."

My mouth went as dry as the desert when he yanked the T-shirt he was wearing over his head.

Noah was completely healed, and the only thing I could see was hard muscle covered by smooth, silken skin.

God, he was so beautiful. His body was so powerful, so hard and unyielding, his spirit so tenacious and strong.

He's officially going to be mine soon.

"You have a problem with that?" he asked, his expression very, very wicked.

I pulled the cotton shirt I was wearing over my head. "Not a single one that I can think of."

I shot him a seductive smile as I unclipped my bra and tossed it aside.

Raw need was starting to claw at me from the inside out.

He came down on the bed and pinned me beneath him, his hand threading through my hair.

My breath seized in my lungs as he looked at me. "I love you, Andie. I promise that I'll try to do everything in my power to make you happy."

Our eyes caught and held, and my heartbeat skittered. "You don't have to try. You already do."

EPILOGUE

ANDIE

Ten months later . . .

"It's finally over," I said to Noah with relief as we ambled down a Boston sidewalk, hand in hand.

Just like he'd promised, Noah had been there with me for my final check with my doctors in Boston.

Because I was so healthy, I hadn't been all that nervous, but Noah had been pretty tense about the whole thing for the last few weeks.

He squeezed my hand. "Thank fuck," he said fiercely. "Not that I suspected anything wrong, but I don't know how the hell you did this so many times."

I shrugged. "A person does what they have to do. But the checks are over. I'm pretty much normal again."

"Baby, you'll never be normal. A fact that I'm actually grateful for, to tell you the truth."

I laughed. "You love it. Who else would find you the best food in every city?"

The man embraced and adored my quirks, just like I did his.

For example, our wedding had been unconventional, but he'd seemed to enjoy every moment of our time in Napa.

The big reception in Citrus Beach had ended up being a beach party. Okay, maybe a very lavish beach party, but we'd had so much fun. Great family. Great friends. Great food. I couldn't have asked for a better day.

"Your idiosyncrasies definitely keep me on my toes," he teased. "There's nothing I don't love about you, Andie. I never want to see you change."

I sighed, thinking about our honeymoon in Europe. We'd started there, and ended up hitting most of the major cities. We'd had an extended honeymoon, but eventually we'd both ended up working a little more once we got back.

Still, Noah never let his work get out of hand, and neither did I. I'd cut my travel back and started working on some investigative stories that I could do closer to home. I hadn't sold any of them yet. I was known for my travel articles, and I had never completed my journalism degree, but I was working on that as well by attending classes at the local university.

I'd never stop writing my blog, or finding new and fantastic places to eat, but I'd always wanted to be an investigative journalist, and Noah had encouraged me to reach for that long-ago goal.

I bumped against his shoulder. "Thank you for being here for me."

I meant that in so many ways, not just this trip to Boston. He'd been there to encourage me in anything I wanted to accomplish.

"You do the same for me," he reminded me.

It was true. Noah and I always encouraged each other like there was no goal either one of us couldn't reach.

Noah was hands-on with his fortune now, and looking for new investments every day. The man had a knack for finding great early investments, especially in technology.

"We're stopping here," Noah said as he halted.

I stopped because he had a firm grip on my hand. "This is my jewelry store," I said, although it was unnecessary. He obviously knew.

He opened the door for me, exactly the same way Owen had a year ago.

"I didn't order anything," I said, looking at him with confusion as the owner waved at me and went into the back of the store. "Since it's all over, I thought that the five bracelets were enough?"

"I'm thinking six is a better number," he said, seeming annoyingly tranquil.

I eyed him suspiciously. "What did you do?"

He didn't have a chance to answer. The owner came rushing out of the back room with a velvet box in her hand. "The best one yet," she said in a pleased voice as she handed me the box.

I looked at Noah. "Open it," he instructed, not giving me a hint of what was inside.

I grasped the lid and exposed the contents.

The bracelet was breathtaking, and I let out a gasp of surprise as I looked at the entwined platinum, rose gold, yellow gold, and white gold. It sparkled because there were encrusted diamonds interspersed across the metal.

My hand shook as I put a finger on it to turn the small engraved plate toward me.

It only had one word, just like all of the other bracelets, but that one word meant everything to me.

Forever.

That was the engraved message, and I knew this bracelet symbolized both an ending and a beginning.

"Oh, my God," I said breathlessly as I carefully lifted the sparkling circle out of the box. "It's so beautiful."

Tears were forming in my eyes as Noah groaned, "Please don't cry. It's a good thing, right?"

I beamed at him, tears shining in my eyes. "It's perfect."

I slipped the bracelet over my hand and loved the sound of the metal jingling against all of the others that had been placed there before it.

Noah tipped my chin up and swiped a tear that escaped from the corner of my eye. "I think you needed this one to complete the set."

I put my hands on his shoulders, and looked at the final bracelet he'd gifted me. "I didn't just need this bracelet, Noah Sinclair. I've always needed you."

He grinned down at me. "Now you have me, and a new bracelet to complete the whole collection."

I nodded as I pulled his head down to kiss him.

I didn't know what force of nature had put Noah in my path so I could find him, but I wasn't going to question my fate.

We belonged together, and we *finally* had our *forever*.

As our lips touched, and I felt the warmth of Noah's love and devotion, I knew that even though we'd both traveled a long road to each other, I'd eventually gotten everything my heart had always wanted . . . and he had been well worth the wait.

ACKNOWLEDGMENTS

I'd like to give a big shout-out to my team at Montlake Romance, and to Maria Gomez, my senior editor. All of you have made my entire journey with Montlake a fantastic experience. I can hardly believe I'll be working on the last book in the Accidental Billionaires series shortly. Where did the time go?

As always, many thanks to my husband, Sri, and my KA team, the people who keep everything going smoothly while I'm buried in my writing cave.

I can never end a book without thanking my readers. I appreciate you so much. Thank you for allowing me to do what I love to do for a living. It's a dream come true for me.

xxxx Jan

ABOUT THE AUTHOR

J.S. "Jan" Scott is the *New York Times* and *USA Today* bestselling author of numerous contemporary and paranormal romances, including the Sinclairs novels and *Ensnared, Entangled,* and *Enamored* in the Accidental Billionaires series. She's an avid reader of all types of books and literature, but romance has always been her genre of choice—so she writes what she loves to read: stories that are almost always steamy, generally feature an alpha male, and have a happily ever after, because she just can't seem to write them any other way! Jan loves to connect with readers. Visit her website at www.authorjsscott.com.

Photo © 2013 Carrie Herzog